International

LUCY

Harlequin Romance®

present

a brand-new miniseries

The Rinucci Brothers

Love, marriage...and a family reunited

The Rinucci brothers: some are related by blood, some not—but Hope Rinucci thinks of all of them as her sons.

Life has dealt each brother a different hand—some are happy, some are troubled—but all are handsome, attractive, successful men, wherever they are in the world.

Meet Justin, Primo and Luke as they find love, marriage—and each other....

Justin's story, *Wife and Mother Forever*—
on sale February 2006, #3879

Primo's story, *Her Italian Boss's Agenda*—
on sale March 2006, #3883

Luke's story, *The Wedding Arrangement*—
on sale April 2006, #3887

Harlequin Romance®

presents

international bestselling author

LUCY GORDON

Readers all over the world love Lucy Gordon for powerful emotional drama, spine-tingling intensity and Italian heroes! Her storytelling talent has won her countless awards—including two RITA® Awards!

About *For the Sake of His Child*

"An outstanding book that not only deals with some very tough issues, but also has layered conflict, a strong premise and fantastic characters."
—*Romantic Times BOOKclub*

About *Bride by Choice*

"An emotionally intense must-read with larger-than-life characters and a heart-wrenching conflict."
—*Romantic Times BOOKclub*

About *The Italian Millionaire's Marriage*

"Lucy Gordon pens an outstanding story. The characters are simply magical, the dialogue is witty and fun and the scenes are just so charming you can't help but smile."
—*Romantic Times BOOKclub*

THE WEDDING ARRANGEMENT

Lucy Gordon

The Rinucci Brothers

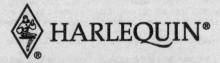

HARLEQUIN®

TORONTO • NEW YORK • LONDON
AMSTERDAM • PARIS • SYDNEY • HAMBURG
STOCKHOLM • ATHENS • TOKYO • MILAN • MADRID
PRAGUE • WARSAW • BUDAPEST • AUCKLAND

ISBN 0-373-03887-9

THE WEDDING ARRANGEMENT

First North American Publication 2006.

Copyright © 2006 by Lucy Gordon.

All rights reserved. Except for use in any review, the reproduction or utilization of this work in whole or in part in any form by any electronic, mechanical or other means, now known or hereafter invented, including xerography, photocopying and recording, or in any information storage or retrieval system, is forbidden without the written permission of the publisher, Harlequin Enterprises Limited, 225 Duncan Mill Road, Don Mills, Ontario, Canada M3B 3K9.

All characters in this book have no existence outside the imagination of the author and have no relation whatsoever to anyone bearing the same name or names. They are not even distantly inspired by any individual known or unknown to the author, and all incidents are pure invention.

This edition published by arrangement with Harlequin Books S.A.

® and TM are trademarks of the publisher. Trademarks indicated with ® are registered in the United States Patent and Trademark Office, the Canadian Trade Marks Office and in other countries.

www.eHarlequin.com

Printed in U.S.A.

Lucy Gordon cut her writing teeth on magazine journalism, interviewing many of the world's most interesting men, including Warren Beatty, Richard Chamberlain, Roger Moore, Sir Alec Guinness and Sir John Gielgud. She also camped out with lions in Africa, and had many other unusual experiences that have often provided the background for her books. She is married to a Venetian, whom she met while on holiday in Venice. They got engaged within two days.

Two of her books have won the Romance Writers of America RITA® award: *Song of the Lorelei* in 1990, and *His Brother's Child* in 1998 in the Best Traditional Romance category.

You can visit her Web site at www.lucy-gordon.com

Books by Lucy Gordon

HARLEQUIN ROMANCE®
3816—HIS PRETEND WIFE
3831—THE MONTE CARLO PROPOSAL
3843—A FAMILY FOR KEEPS
3855—THE ITALIAN'S RIGHTFUL BRIDE
3879—WIFE AND MOTHER FOREVER*
3883—THE ITALIAN BOSS'S AGENDA*

*The Rinucci Brothers

CHAPTER ONE

I'M CRAZY to leave.

The words pounded in Luke Cayman's head as he packed his bags on the day after his brother Primo's engagement.

I should stay and fight for her.

Yet he got into his brand new state-of-the-art sports car and headed out of Naples 'like a bat out of hell', as he put it.

It was a relief to get on to the *autostrada*, where he could let it rip, driving the two hundred miles to Rome at the top of the legal limit and making it in two and a half hours.

Once there, he checked into a five-star hotel in Parioli, the wealthiest and most elegant part of the city, and indulged himself with the best of Roman cuisine and wine, which he drank in brooding silence.

I should have stayed.

But there was Olympia's face in his mind, as he'd last seen it, her eyes fixed blissfully on Primo, her fiancé, soon to be her husband. Who was he trying to kid? He'd never stood a chance.

He was just thinking of an early night when a hand clapped him on the shoulder and a hearty voice said, 'You should have told me you were coming.'

Bernardo was the hotel manager, a plump, hearty man in his mid-forties. Luke had stayed here before on business trips to Rome, and they had always been on good terms.

'It was a last-minute decision,' Luke said, trying to sound cheerful. 'I find myself the owner of a building in Rome and it needs my attention.'

'Property? I thought you were in manufacturing.'

'I am. This place was given to me in repayment of a debt.'

'Round here?'

'No, Trastevere.'

Bernardo raised his eyebrows. If Parioli was Rome's most elegant area, Trastevere was its most colourful.

'I gather it's in a poor state of repair,' Luke said. 'When I've put it right, I'll sell it.'

'Why not just sell it now? Let someone else bother with the repairs.'

'Signora Pepino would never let me get away with that,' Luke said with a grin. 'She's a lawyer who lives and works there, and has already bombarded me with letters saying what she expects me to do.'

'And you'll do what this woman tells you?'

'She isn't a woman, she's a dragon. That's why I didn't tell her I was coming. I can get a look at the place before she starts breathing fire at me.'

'Is that the only reason?' Bernardo asked, regarding him shrewdly.

Luke shrugged.

'Ah, a lovely lady broke your heart and now—'

'No woman has ever broken my heart,' Luke said sharply. 'I don't allow that to happen.'

'Very wise.'

'I let myself get a little too close to a woman, although

I knew she was in love with another man. It was a mistake, but mistakes can be put right. A wise man sees the danger and takes action.'

'And you managed that with your customary efficiency?'

'My what?'

'You're known as a man who believes in good order, keeps things in proportion, and stays invulnerable. I envy you. It must make life simple. But now you need to get blissfully roaring drunk, with good companions who will put you safely to bed afterwards.'

'For pity's sake, Bernardo, how often have you seen me like that?'

'Not often enough. It's unnatural.'

Luke gave a reluctant laugh. 'Maybe, but it helps a man stay in charge of his life, and that's what matters. Goodnight.'

He went to his room quickly, suddenly uneasy in Bernardo's company. For a moment he'd seen himself through his friend's eyes, a man who prized good order and self-control above all else: a cold, hard man, who gave little and counted it out carefully first.

It wasn't so far from the truth, he thought. But it had never troubled him before.

He checked the messages on his cellphone and the words, *Call your mother,* appeared on the screen. Grinning, he called Hope Rinucci, his adoptive mother, and the only one he had known.

'Hi, Mamma. Yes, I got here safely. Everything's fine.'

'Have you met Signora Pepino yet?'

'I've barely arrived. I've had a meal, that's all. Let me settle in before I confront her. I need all my courage.'

His mother's exasperated voice reached him down the line. 'Don't pretend you're afraid of her.'

'I am. I'm shaking in my shoes, I swear it.'

'You'll go to hell for telling lies, and serve you right.'

He chuckled. She always made him feel better.

In his mind he could see her in the Villa Rinucci, high up on the hill. She liked to take phone calls on the terrace, looking out over the Bay of Naples, the most glorious view in the world, according to her. It would be dark now, with only the twinkling lights breaking through the black velvet, but the beauty was still there.

'Are you exhausted after all the festivities?' he asked.

'I've no time for that. I'm planning the party for Primo and Olympia's engagement.'

'I thought we had that last night.'

'No, that was just the tail end of Justin's wedding,' she said, naming her first son. 'One wedding begets another, and naturally we toasted Primo and Olympia, but they'll want a proper engagement celebration of their own.'

'And if they don't they're going to get it anyway,' he said with wry fondness.

'Well, you can't expect me to pass up the chance of a party,' she said reasonably.

'It would never occur to me that you'd pass up the chance of a party,' he said truthfully. 'And after that, there's the wedding, unless Olympia's mother has some mad idea of organising it herself.'

'Oh, no, we discussed that last night, and she quite agrees with me.'

'You mean she can't stand up to you any more than the rest of us,' he said with a laugh.

'I don't know what you mean,' Hope said, affronted. And she really didn't.

'I look forward to it. I won't miss the chance to gloat over brother Primo's downfall.'

'You'll meet the right one for you,' Hope said, like all mothers.

'Maybe not. I might just settle for being a curmudgeonly old bachelor.'

Hope crowed with laughter. 'A handsome boy like you?'

'Boy? I'm thirty-eight.'

'You'll always be a boy to me. Your wife is next on my list, and don't you forget it. Now, go and have a good time.'

'Mamma, it's eleven o'clock.'

'So? The perfect time for—anything you want.'

Luke grinned. His mother had never been a prude—one reason why her sons adored her. Toni, her husband, was far more strait-laced.

'I need to be clear-headed to deal with Signora Pepino.'

'Nonsense! Just turn your charm on her, and that'll do the trick.'

Hope Rinucci was convinced that all her sons had the charm of the devil and no woman could resist them. With the younger ones it was possibly true, but Luke knew that charm wasn't his strong suit. He was a tall, muscular, well-made man with features that were regular enough to pass for good looks. But his face fell naturally into stern lines and he smiled little.

It had been different with Olympia. In the few weeks he'd shared his apartment with her he'd forced himself to behave like a gentleman, knowing that her heart was already given to his brother, Primo. It hadn't been easy keeping his infatuation under control, and the strain had almost propelled it into outright love.

He knew that under Olympia's influence his nature had thawed, almost to the point of charm. But he was on his guard against it happening for a second time. Authority, no-nonsense, stubbornness: these he did well. Not charm.

But since there was no arguing with a mother's partiality he didn't try. They finished the conversation affectionately and he hung up, feeling strangely uneasy again. Something was wrong. He didn't know what, but he had an uncomfortable sense that the trouble lay with himself.

As always, when something disturbed him, he took refuge in work, pulling out the folder that contained the details of his newly acquired, if unwanted, property.

It was called the Residenza Gallini, a grandiose name that presumably promised more than it delivered, and, from the plan, seemed to be a five-storey building, built around four sides of a courtyard. The heart of the folder was the correspondence with Signora Minerva Pepino, a severe and ferocious lady whose very name was beginning to worry him.

It was easy fighting a man. You could go in with fists flailing. With a woman subtlety was needed, and Luke, who didn't 'do' subtlety any more than he 'did' charm, felt at a disadvantage.

She had opened hostilities with a reasonably restrained letter enquiring when he intended to come to Rome and set in motion the vast amount of work that was necessary to bring the property up to the standard essential to her clients, who lived there in conditions that were a disgrace.

He had replied assuring her that he would arrive 'as soon as was convenient' and venturing, in the mildest possible way, to suggest that she exaggerated the conditions.

She had treated his mildness with the contempt it deserved, blasting him with a list of necessary repairs and including the probable prices, whose total made him gulp.

But now he felt he was getting her measure. The tradesmen who'd given these estimates were probably friends or relatives, and she was on commission. He began to be offended at the way she clearly thought she could bully him, and repeated his assurance that he would come to Rome when it was convenient.

And so it had gone on, each growing more quellingly polite as their annoyance rose. Luke imagined her as a woman carved out of granite, probably in her fifties, ruling her world with grim efficiency, crushing all disagreement. Even her name was alarming. Minerva was the goddess of wisdom, known for her brilliant intellect but also for being born wearing armour and wielding a spear.

He would visit Rome and act like a responsible landlord. What he would not do was let himself be ordered around.

He put the folder away. Suddenly his room felt too quiet, its very luxury pressing in on him like a stifling blanket. Coming to a sudden decision, he took the cash out of his wallet and put it in his pocket along with the plastic card that was the key to his room. Then he locked the wallet in the wall safe, and headed downstairs.

It was a balmy night and he was warm enough in his

shirtsleeves as he walked away from the hotel and hailed a taxi to take him the length of the Via del Corso, with its late-night cafés and glittering shops. At the bottom they swung right, heading for the Garibaldi Bridge over the River Tiber.

'Here will do,' he called to the driver when they had crossed the river.

He knew now that he must have reached the part of Rome known as Trastevere, a name which literally meant 'on the other side of the Tiber'. It was the oldest part of the city, and still the most colourful. The light streamed on to the streets, accompanied by song, laughter and appetising smells of cooking.

He plunged into the nearest bar and was soon enveloped in conviviality. From there he drifted to another bar, relaxed by some of the best local wine he had ever tasted. Three bars later he was beginning to think that this was the way to live.

He wandered out into the cobbled street and stood there, gazing up at the full moon. Then he studied the street, realising that he had no idea where he was.

'Looking for something?'

Turning, he saw a young man sitting at one of the outside tables. He was little more than a boy, with a charming, mobile face and dark, vivid eyes. When he grinned his teeth flashed with almost startling brilliance.

'Ciao!' he said, raising his glass in tipsy fellowship.

'Ciao!' Luke answered, coming to sit at the table beside him. 'I was just realising that I'm lost.'

'New here?'

'Just arrived today.'

'Well, now you're here, you should stay. Nice place. Nice people.'

Luke signalled to a waiter, who brought two fresh glasses and a full bottle, accepted Luke's money and departed.

'*Very* nice people,' the boy repeated.

'I probably shouldn't have done that,' Luke said, suddenly conscience-stricken. 'I think you've already had enough.'

'If the wine is good, there's no such thing as enough.' He filled both glasses. 'Soon I shall have had too much, and it still won't be enough.' A thought struck him. 'I'm a very wise man. At least, I sound like one.'

'Well, I guess it makes a kind of sense,' Luke agreed, tasting the wine and finding it good. 'I'm Luke, by the way.'

The young man frowned. 'Luke? Lucio?'

'Sure, Lucio if you want.'

'I'm Charlie.'

It was Luke's turn to frown. An Italian called Charlie?

'You mean Carlo?' he asked at last.

'No, Charlie. It's short for Charlemagne.' The boy added confidentially, 'I don't tell many people that, only my very best friends.'

'Thank you,' Luke said, accepting the honour with a grin. 'So tell your friend why you were named after the Emperor Charlemagne.'

'Because I'm descended from him, of course.'

'But he lived twelve hundred years ago. How can you be sure?'

Charlie looked surprised. 'My mother told me.'

'And you believe everything your mother tells you?'

'What Mamma says, you'd better believe, or you'll be sorry.'

'Yes, mine's that way too,' Luke said, grinning.

They clinked glasses, and Charlie drained his, then quickly refilled it.

'I drink to forget,' he announced gleefully.

'Forget what?'

'Something or other. Who cares? Why do you drink?'

'I'm trying to nerve myself to confront a dragon. Otherwise she might eat me.'

'Ah, a female dragon. They're the worst. But you'll slay her.'

'I don't think this lady is easily intimidated.'

'You just tell her you're not standing for any nonsense,' Charlie advised. 'That's the way to deal with women.'

So now he had two pieces of advice for dealing with the situation—use his non-existent charm, or try to impose what this naïve boy fondly imagined to be 'masculine authority'.

They passed on to the next bar, and then the next, until it began to feel like time to go home.

Suddenly they heard a shout from the next street, then the sound of a child crying and an animal squealing and suddenly a crowd of young men came stumbling out of the shadows. The one in front was carrying a puppy that was squirming to escape. With them was a boy of about twelve, who continually tried to rescue his pet, but was thwarted as the lout tossed the puppy to one of the others.

'Bastardi!' Charlie exclaimed violently.

'I couldn't agree more,' Luke said.

They moved forward together.

The sight of them made the louts pause just long enough for Charlie to seize the puppy. Two of them tried to snatch it back, but Luke occupied them long enough for Charlie to give the animal to the child, who grabbed it and vanished, leaving him free to concentrate on the fight.

Two against four might seem an unequal conquest, but Charlie was furious and Luke was powerful and they managed to stop them chasing the fleeing child until there were further sounds from the narrow alleys, shouts, sirens, and all six were surrounded and carted off to the nearest police station.

The knock on the door could only be Mamma Netta Pepino. Nobody else knocked in exactly that pattern and Minnie was smiling as she went to answer it.

'It isn't too late?' Netta asked at once.

'No, I hadn't gone to bed.'

'Every night you stay up late, working too hard. So I brought you some shopping because I know you don't have time to do your own.'

This was a fiction that they had shared for years. Minnie had an expensive law practice on the Via Veneto, and a secretary who could have done her shopping. But the habit of relying on Netta had started years ago, when she had been eighteen, the bride of Gianni Pepino, and this warm, laughing woman had embraced her.

It had been that way through the years when Minnie studied law, and had continued as her practice built up to its present success. Gianni had been dead for four years now, but Minnie had neither moved to a more luxurious home, nor weakened her links to Netta, whom she loved as a mother.

'Proscuitto, Parmesan, pasta—your favourite kind,' Netta intoned, dumping bags on the table. 'You check.'

'No need, you always get it right,' Minnie said with a smile. 'Sit down and have a drink. Coffee? Whisky?'

'Whisky,' Netta said with a chuckle, heaving her huge person into a chair.

'I'll have some tea.'

'You're still English,' Netta said. 'Fourteen years you live in Italy and you still drink English tea.'

Minnie began putting the shopping away, pausing as she came to a small bunch of flowers.

'I thought you'd like them,' Netta said, elaborately casual.

'I love them,' Minnie said, dropping a kiss on her cheek. 'Let's put them with Gianni.'

Filling a small vase with water, she added the flowers and set it beside a photograph of Gianni that stood on a shelf. It had been taken a week before his death and showed a young man with a wide, humorous mouth and brilliant eyes that seemed to have a gleam deep in their depths. His naturally curly hair was too long, falling over his forehead and down his neck, and increasing the charm that glowed from the picture.

Next to him stood another picture, of a young girl. Once she had been the eighteen-year-old Minnie, her face soft, slightly unfinished, still full of hope. She hadn't known grief and despair. That came later.

Her face was finer now, elegant, more withdrawn, but still open to humour. Her fair hair, worn long in the first picture, now just brushed her shoulders, a length chosen for efficient management.

She changed the position of the flowers twice before she was satisfied.

'He will like that,' Netta said. 'Always he loves flowers. Remember how often he brought them to you? Flowers for your wedding, flowers for your birthday, your anniversary—'

'Yes, he never forgot.'

Neither woman thought it strange to speak of him both in the present and the past, changing from sentence to sentence. It came so naturally that they barely noticed.

'How's Poppa?' Minnie asked.

'Always he complains.'

'No change there, then.' They laughed together.

'And Charlie?'

Netta groaned at the mention of her younger son. 'He's a bad boy. He thinks he's a big man because he stays out late and drinks too much and sees too many girls.'

'So he's a normal eighteen-year-old,' Minnie said gently.

In fact she, too, had been growing a little uneasy at her young brother-in-law's exuberant habits, but she played it down for Netta's sake.

'It was better when he was in love with you,' Netta mourned.

'Mamma, he wasn't in love with me. He's eighteen, I'm thirty-two. He had a boyish crush, which I defused. At least, I hope I did. Charlie's of no interest to me.'

'No man interests you. It's not natural. You're a beautiful woman.'

'I'm a widow.'

'For too long. Now it's time.'

'This is my mother-in-law talking?' Minnie asked of nobody in particular.

'This is a woman talking to a woman. Four years you are a widow, yet no man. *Scandoloso!*'

'It's not quite true to say there have been no men in my life,' Minnie said cautiously. 'And, since you live right opposite me, you know that.'

'Sure. I see them come and I see them go. But I don't see them stay.'

'I don't invite them to stay,' Minnie said quietly.

Netta's answer to this was to give her a crushing hug.

'No man ever had a better wife than my Gianni,' she said. 'Now it's time you think of yourself. You need a man in your life, in your bed.'

'Netta, please—'

'When I was your age I had—'

'A husband and five children,' Minnie reminded her.

'That's true, but—ah, well, it was a long time ago.'

Netta had a generous nature. In all things.

'I'm quite happy without a man,' Minnie insisted.

'Nonsense. No woman is happy without a man.'

'And, even if I wanted one, it wouldn't be Charlie. I'm not a cradle-robber.'

'Of course not. But you could make him listen. Where is he tonight? I don't know. But I'm sure he's with bad people.'

'And I'm sure that when you get home you'll find him there looking sheepish,' Minnie assured her.

'Then I go home now. And I tell him he should be ashamed for worrying his mother.'

'I'll tell him, too. Come on, I'll walk home with you.'

Minnie's home was on the third floor, overlooking the courtyard. Some of the other homes were also occupied by Pepinos, since the family had always liked to live within hailing distance of each other. As they went out on to the iron staircase that ran around the inside of the courtyard, they could see lights in the other windows and shadows passing across them.

Then, up the stairs to the fourth floor on the other side, to the front door of the home Netta shared with her husband, her brother and her youngest son, when he was at home. There was still no sign of Charlie.

'He'll be home soon,' Minnie said soothingly. 'He's just trying his wings.'

She kissed her mother-in-law and wandered back to her own little apartment. As always, it felt very quiet when she let herself in. It had been that way since the day her young husband had died in her arms.

She was suddenly very tired. Netta's conversation had steered her close to things she normally tried not to think of.

From his place on the shelf Gianni seemed to follow her around the apartment with his eyes. She smiled at him, trying to find reassurance in his presence as she had so often before. But this time she couldn't sense him smiling back.

The kitchen table was scattered with papers. Reluctantly she sat down to finish her work, but her mind couldn't concentrate. It was a relief when her cellphone rang.

'Charlie! Mamma's been worrying about you. Where have you got to? You're *where*?'

CHAPTER TWO

THE young policeman looked up with admiration as Signora Minerva strode into the station.

'*Buona notte,*' he said. 'It's always a pleasure to see you here, *signora.*'

'Be careful, Rico,' she warned him. 'That remark could be construed as harassment. You're reminding me that my relatives are always in some sort of trouble.'

'No, I was saying how pretty you always look,' he replied, hurt.

Minnie laughed. She liked Rico, a naïve country boy, overwhelmed by his assignment to Rome, and wide-eyed about everything, including herself.

'Always?' she teased.

'Every time your relatives are in trouble,' he said irrepressibly. 'How an important lawyer like yourself comes to be related to so many criminals—'

'That's enough!' she told him sternly. 'I grant you, they can be a little wayward, but there's never anything violent.'

'Signor Charlie has been in something violent tonight. His shirt is torn, he's bleeding. Huge big fight. The fellow with him is even worse. He's a big, bad man with a nasty face.' Rico took a deep breath as he came to the real crime. 'And he doesn't have any papers.'

'What, nothing?'

'No identity card. No passport.'

'Well, we don't all carry our passports around with us.'

'But this man speaks Italian with an accent. He is a foreigner.' He added in a low, horrified voice, 'I think he's English.'

'So was my mother,' Minnie said sharply. 'It's not a hanging crime.'

'But he has no papers,' Rico said, returning to the heart of the matter. 'And he won't say where he's living, so he's probably sleeping in the streets. Very drunk.'

'And he was fighting Charlie?'

'No, they were on the same side—I think. It's hard to be sure because Charlie's drunk too.'

'Where is he?'

'In a cell, with this other fellow. I think he's afraid of him. He won't say a word against him.'

'Does "this fellow" have a name?'

'He won't give his name, but Charlie calls him Lucio. I'll take you to him.'

She knew the way to the cells by now, having come here so often to help her relatives, who were as light-fingered as they were light-hearted. Even so, she was aghast at the sight of her young brother-in-law, seated lolling against the wall, scruffy, bruised and definitely the worse for wear.

Rico vanished to find the key, which he'd forgotten to bring. Minnie stood watching Charlie, wishing he didn't look so much like a down-and-out. But his companion was even worse, she realised, as though he'd fought ten men.

Tall, muscular, unshaven, he looked strong enough to deal with any number of opponents. Like Charlie he wore a badly torn shirt and his face was bruised, with a cut over one eye. But, unlike Charlie, he didn't look as if it were all too much for him. In fact, he didn't look as though anything would be too much for him.

So this was Lucio, a thoroughly ugly customer, brutal, with huge fists to power his way through the world—a man used to getting his own way by the use of force. She gave a shudder of distaste.

Then Charlie seemed to half wake up, rub his eyes, lean forward with his hands between his knees and his head bent in an attitude of dejection. 'Lucio' came to sit beside him and put a hand on his shoulder, shaking him slightly in a rallying manner.

Charlie said something that she couldn't catch and Lucio replied. He, too, was inaudible, but she sensed that he spoke gently. Then he grinned, and the sight surprised her. It was ribald and full of derision, yet with a hint of kindness, and it seemed to hearten the boy.

Rico returned. 'I'll let him out and you can talk with him in an interview room,' he said, 'well away from that one.'

The sound of the key turning made both men look up. Rico opened the door and addressed Charlie in a portentous tone.

'Signor Pepino, your sister is here. Also your lawyer.' Trying to be witty, he added, 'They came together.'

Out of the corner of her eye Minnie saw Lucio stiffen and throw a sharp look at Charlie, then at her. He stared as though thunderstruck. His eyes contained both a frown and a question as they looked her up and down in a considering way that was almost insulting.

In this she did him an injustice. Luke was beyond thinking anything except that this couldn't possibly be happening.

Pepino? A lawyer?

She was Signora Pepino? This dainty fair-haired creature was the dragon? And he, who'd laid such plans for gaining the upper hand, found himself in a police cell—

dishevelled, disorderly, hung-over and, worst of all, dependent on her.

Great!

Charlie tried to fling his arms about her, hailing her emotionally as his saviour.

'Get off, you ruffian!' she told him firmly. 'You look as if you've been rolling in the gutter and you smell like a brewery. I suppose you're relying on me to get you out of here?'

'And my friend,' Charlie said, indicating Luke.

'Your friend will wish to make his own arrangements.'

'No, I've told him you'll look after him too. He saved my life, Minnie. You wouldn't abandon him to his fate when he's poor and alone and has nobody to help him?' Charlie was in an ecstasy of tipsy emotion.

Minnie groaned. 'If you don't shut up I'll abandon *you*,' she told him in exasperation.

'I'll take you to an interview room,' Rico said.

'No, thank you, I'll stay here and talk to both of them.'

'Stay here?' Rico asked, aghast. 'With that one?' He pointed to Luke.

'I'm not afraid of him,' she said crossly. 'Perhaps *he* should be afraid of *me*. How dare you do this to my brother?'

Luke leaned against the wall, regarding her ironically through half-closed eyes.

'Look,' he said, sounding bored, 'bail your brother out or do what you have to. Then go. I can manage for myself.'

'Lucio, no!' Charlie exclaimed. 'Minnie, you must look after him. He's my friend.'

'He's a lot older than you and should know better,' she said firmly.

'That's right, it's all my fault,' Luke said. 'Just leave.'

He promised himself that when they next met he would be washed, shaved and well-pressed. With any luck she might not even recognise him.

'What did you mean about saving your life?' she asked.

Charlie launched into an explanation which was more or less accurate considering the state he was in. The word 'puppy' occurred several times and by the end Minnie had a rough idea that the stranger had come between Charlie and superior odds, although perhaps not as melodramatically as he described it.

'Is that what happened?' she asked Luke in a gentler tone.

'Something like that. Neither Charlie nor I like seeing a child bullied. Or a puppy,' he added after a moment.

'What happened to the child?'

'Grabbed the puppy and ran. Then there was a bit more fighting, and someone must have called the police.'

'Well, I'm glad you were there with Charlie, Signor—'

'Lucio will do,' he said hastily.

'But I can't represent you if I don't know your name.'

'I haven't asked you to represent me.' Inspiration made him add, 'I can't afford a lawyer.'

'It'll be my gift, to show my gratitude.'

Luke groaned, mentally imploring heaven to save him from a woman who had an answer to everything!

'As Charlie says, I can't just abandon you,' Minnie went on. 'But you must be quite frank with me. Where are you living?'

'Nowhere,' he said hastily, imagining her mirth if he gave the name of the hotel.

'Sleeping in the streets?'

'That's right.'

'But it makes my job harder. So does your lack of identity. How come you don't have an ID card?'

'I do.'

'Where?'

'I left it in the hotel,' he said before he could stop himself.

'But you just said you were sleeping in the streets.'

'I'm not at my best,' he said, inwardly cursing her alertness. 'I don't know what I'm saying.'

'Signor—whatever your name is, I don't think you're as drunk as all that, and I don't like clients who mess me around. Please tell me the name of your hotel.'

'The Contini.'

Silence.

She looked him up and down, taking in every scruffy, dishevelled detail.

'All right, you're a comedian,' she said. 'Very funny. Now, will you please tell me where you're staying?'

'I just did. I can't help it if you don't believe me.'

'The most expensive hotel in Rome? Would *you* believe you, looking the way you do?'

'I didn't come out looking like this. I left everything behind in case of pickpockets.' He looked down at his disreputable self. 'Now I don't suppose any pickpocket would bother with me.'

'*If* you are telling the truth, and I'm not sure I believe it, I still need your name.'

He sighed. There was no help for it.

'Luke Cayman.'

For a moment Minnie didn't move. She was frowning as though trying to understand something.

'What did you say?' she asked at last.

'Luke Cayman.'

She drummed her fingers. 'Is that a joke?'

'Why would you think so?' he fenced.

'I thought maybe I'd heard the name before, but perhaps I was mistaken.'

'No, I don't think you were,' he said deliberately.

They regarded each other, each with roughly the same mixture of exasperation and incredulity. Charlie looked blank, understanding nothing.

Suddenly his expression changed and he took a deep breath. In a flash Minnie was at the door, calling for Rico, who came running.

'You'd better get him out quickly,' she said.

Rico did so, guiding Charlie down the corridor to where he could be ill in peace.

'Let's get this settled,' Minnie said. 'I do not believe that you're Luke Cayman.'

'Why? Because I don't fit your preconceived notion? You don't fit mine, but I'm willing to be tolerant.'

'You think this is very funny—'

'Well, no, this isn't how I'd have chosen to meet you. With a bit of conniving I dare say you could get me locked up for years. Look me in the eye and say you aren't tempted.'

'Well, I'm not,' she snapped. 'It's the last thing I want.'

'Very virtuous of you.'

'Virtuous, nothing!' she said, goaded into candour. 'With you locked up, the Residenza would be in limbo, with no hope of getting anything done. You may be sure I'll do my best to make you a free man.'

'I see. If anyone's going to give me grief, you'd prefer it to be you.'

'Exactly.'

Charlie returned, looking pale but slightly better, and

glanced back and forth between them, sensing strain in the air.

'We were discussing strategy,' Minnie said.

'I've decided not to hire you,' Luke told her. 'I'd feel safer if you just leave me to my fate.'

'No,' Charlie burst out. 'Minnie's a good lawyer; she'll get you out of trouble.'

'Only because she's got far more trouble planned for me,' Luke said with a derisive grin.

'Please, let's not be melodramatic,' Minnie said coolly. 'I shall treat you exactly as I would any other client.'

'You see?' Charlie urged. 'Honestly, Lucio, she's the best. They call her the "giant slayer" because she'll take on anyone and win. You should see the battle she's preparing for the monster who owns our building.'

'I can imagine,' Luke murmured. 'A monster, eh?'

'Yes, but she's says he's going to die a horrible death,' Charlie said with relish.

'Literally, or only legally?' Luke asked with interest.

'Whichever seems necessary,' Minnie said, meeting his eyes.

'I gather you'll make that decision at a later date.'

'I like to keep my options open.'

'When she's finished he'll wish he'd never been born,' Charlie added.

'Does this monster have a name?' Luke asked with interest.

'No, Minnie just calls him the "devil incarnate".'

'Stop talking nonsense, both of you,' she said severely. 'I've got to work out what we're going to do. You'll be in court in a few hours and you can't go looking like that. Charlie, I'll send someone down with clean clothes for you. Signor Cayman, you'll need fresh clothes, too, and your ID card. How do I get them?'

'I could call the hotel and ask them to arrange it,' he said reluctantly. 'But I don't want them to know I'm here.'

'You're right. Can I get into your room?'

'Yes, I brought the card with me.' From his back pocket he drew the sliver of plastic that acted like a key at the Contini and handed it to her, giving her the code. 'It's on the third floor.'

'I don't believe I'm doing this,' she said, half to him, half to herself.

'Try to forget that I'm the devil incarnate,' he said. 'That should make it easier.'

Charlie looked from one to the other, baffled.

'You can explain it when I'm gone,' she told Luke.

Rico opened the door for her. At the last moment she turned to look back at Luke and said, 'By the way, I didn't call you the devil incarnate.'

'Thank you.'

'I called you "the creature from the black lagoon". I'll see you later.'

Heading north, she swung her car on to the Ponte Sisto, the bridge that would take her over the Tiber in the direction of the Contini Hotel. As she drove, she seethed.

She had been furiously angry for years. The man who'd owned the Residenza had been a reprobate who had resisted her attempts to make him spend money on the property. When she'd moved the law against him he'd always found a way to wriggle out.

And then, just when she'd thought she had him cornered, he'd pulled a final rabbit out of the hat, signing over the building to Luke Cayman, so that she had to start again. It was a moot point whether she were angrier with him or Luke Cayman.

And now, to find herself defending the enemy, was enough to make her explode.

A cool head would dictate placating him, saving him from the gallows—figuratively speaking—then turning on the charm. But she was too incensed to consider it.

By now dawn was breaking, covering the sleeping city with a soft white mist. In the distance she could see the Contini, a huge, luxurious building created from an ancient palazzo. She could hardly believe that the ruffian she had left in the cells was actually staying here.

Luckily the night receptionist was dozing and it was easy to slip past. On the third floor she found Luke's room without trouble. It was large and lavishly appointed, with a balcony.

She went out and stood regarding the view as the light grew brighter. To her right lay the lush green lawns of the Borghese Gardens. To her left she could see the Vatican, the early sun just touching the dome of St Peter's. Between them glided the River Tiber.

It was a marvellous scene, full of peace and beauty.

A rich man's scene, she thought crossly. For only a rich man could afford to stand in this exact spot and see such wonders spread before him. And one particular rich man had thought it amusing to leave his wealth briefly behind and go out slumming it for fun.

He'd got more than he'd bargained for, but in the end he had only to send someone to his expensive hotel, to go through his expensive clothes and put everything expensively right for him. And all the while his tenants lived in a building that was falling apart.

For a moment she was so livid that she almost stormed out, leaving everything behind. Let him take his chances! See how funny he found that!

But her professionalism took over. She would do her job.

She surveyed the suits in his wardrobe until she found one of a dark charcoal colour. To go with it she chose a white shirt and a dark blue silk tie. Then she rummaged in the drawers for clean socks and underpants. As she had more than half expected, he wore boxer shorts.

Well, it wouldn't be a satin thong, she mused with a faint smile. *Not him.*

She packed everything into a bag she found in the wardrobe, then opened the wall safe using the plastic card that had opened the door. Inside she found his wallet and checked it for the ID card. It was there, and so was something else—a photograph of one of the loveliest young women Minnie had ever seen.

She was wearing trousers and standing, leaning against a wall, her thumbs hooked into her belt, one foot up against the wall in a pose that emphasised her height and slender grace.

Like many beautiful women Minnie was fascinated by beauty of a different kind in others. Where she herself was fair, this was a brunette with marvellous dark hair streaming down to her waist, giving her an exotic, mysterious look.

She was also wonderfully tall. As a child Minnie had dreamed of growing to five foot ten and becoming a model. In the end she'd had to settle for five foot four, or 'nothing very much' as she'd crossly put it.

But this was how she'd always longed to be, with legs that went up to her ears and a neck that came from a swan.

'Grr!' she said to the picture. 'Who are you? His wife? His fiancée? Girlfriend? Whoever you are, you've got no right to look like that.'

She replaced the picture carefully in the wallet, which she then put in her own bag, to take to him.

From a distance she heard the bell of St Peter's, chiming seven o'clock, and realised that the light was growing fast, the city was waking and she still had much to do.

She should call Netta, but a quick rummage in her bag revealed that she'd left her cellphone behind. Using the bedside phone might be indiscreet. That left Luke Cayman's own cellphone. After a brief hesitation, she took it and dialled. When Netta answered she kept her tone light.

'Netta? That silly boy has been up to his tricks. He drank too much last night, got into a brawl and he's at the police station.'

She heard Netta give a little shriek and hastened to add, 'Don't worry, I'll sort it. It's not the first time.'

'Oh, Minnie, you will get him out, promise me.'

'Don't I always? But I need you to get down there with some clean clothes so that he can look good in court. It'll just be a fine and when you get him home you can make him sorry he was born.'

After a few more reassurances she hung up. Before putting the phone away, she studied it a little, tempted by its state-of-the-art appearance, and making a mental note to replace her own with one exactly like this beauty.

Nothing but the best for him, she mused.

She was about to switch it off when it rang and, before she could stop herself, she answered it.

'Pronto!'

The action was completely automatic, and only when the word was out did she realise what she'd done.

The caller was a woman, sounding a little surprised at hearing Minnie.

'*Scusi?*' she said. 'Is this Luke Cayman's phone or do I have a wrong number?'

'No, this is his phone. If I could explain—'

The other voice became warm and charming. 'My dear, there's no need for you to explain. I understand perfectly. I should apologise for calling so early, but I overlooked the time. Please ask Luke to call his mother when he can spare a moment.'

'Yes—yes, I'll do that,' Minnie stammered, for once not in control. 'Er—it won't be in the next few minutes, I'm afraid—'

'That's all right. I was once young myself. I'm sure you're extremely beautiful.'

'But—'

'*Ciao!*' The line went dead.

Well, that was that, she thought crossly.

Luke's mother thought she was his girlfriend, rising from the sheets after a night of passion, and about to dive back in for another riotous round of pleasure.

She could have screamed with vexation.

For precisely one minute she sat there, taking deep breaths. Then she finished packing, taking care to switch off the phone before it could ring again, and hurried out of the room, just managing not to slam the door behind her.

At the police station she showed Luke's ID card at the desk before going to the cell.

'There's just the "drunk and disorderly" to deal with, and I assume you have no previous convictions?'

'None,' he assured her.

'You'll go before a Justice of the Peace in a couple of hours. He'll fine you and that'll be the end of it.'

He was looking in the bag she'd brought. 'You've

done a great job. These will make me look like a pillar of the community.'

'Hmm!'

'I won't ask what that means. I'm sure you're longing to tell me.'

'But you're not going to give me the satisfaction. Very wise.'

He declined to answer this, but his harsh face softened and there was briefly a devil in his eyes. Suddenly Minnie remembered his mother's mistaken assumption, and she had a horrid feeling that she might be about to blush.

'I'll see you in court,' she said, and departed with dignity.

Netta returned home with Minnie to cook her some breakfast while she showered, ready for court later that morning.

'Bless you,' she said, emerging in a towelling dressing gown to sit down before muesli and fruit juice. 'Don't worry. Charlie's going to be all right.'

'I know. You'll take care of him like you've done before. And also of that nice young man.'

'Nice—you mean that brute with him? You know nothing about him.'

'Rico let me into the cell to see Charlie, and we all had a talk. I'm glad you are helping him, too.'

'Don't be fooled, Netta. I can see that he's been to work on you, but you needn't feel sorry for him.'

'But of course I must be concerned for the man who saved Charlie's life,' Netta said, scandalised.

'Saved his life, my left foot!' Minnie said with frank derision. 'I don't believe he did any such thing.'

'But Charlie says so,' Netta persisted.

'After what Charlie's taken on board I wouldn't rely on him for the time of day. And I wouldn't rely on this other character for anything. He's our new landlord. The enemy.'

'But he's not our enemy, *cara*. He explained to me how it happened, how he did not want the Residenza—'

'That isn't going to make him a better landlord,' Minnie pointed out.

'He told me that he thought he had offended you, and how he feels most desolate—'

'Did he, indeed?' Minnie said with grim appreciation of these tactics.

'And I said I was eternally grateful to him for saving my Charlie, and he was welcome in our home at any time.'

'You might well say that, since he happens to own it.'

'Then everything is all right.' Netta beamed. 'We are all friends, and he will make the repairs—'

'And double the rent.'

'You will talk to him, be nice, make *him* nice.'

'Netta, listen, this is one very clever man. He's been to work on you, and achieved exactly what he wanted. You're putty in his hands.'

'Twenty years ago, I would have been,' Netta said with a sigh.

Minnie refused to allow her lips to twitch. 'Don't think like that,' she said with an attempt at severity. 'It's just giving in to him.'

'OK, *you* give in to him. Such a man was made for a woman to give in to. Or many women.'

'Then they'd be very foolish. He knows what to say and do, but it's all meaningless. I'd love to know what really happened in this fight.'

'He was defending Charlie and the little puppy—'

'I think he was probably just fighting the puppy,'

Minnie said cynically. 'I expect it bit him. Good for the puppy!'

'Why are you so unkind to the poor man?'

It would have taken too long to explain, so Minnie just said, 'I'll get dressed and we'll go.'

CHAPTER THREE

Two hours later she presented herself before the Justice of the Peace, Alfredo Fentoni, clad in the voluminous black robe of the advocate. Fentoni, who knew her, smiled benignly, addressed her as *Avvocato*, and they began.

Minnie had to admit that Luke was much improved. The suit spoke of sober respectability, and a shave had transformed him into something resembling an ordinary man.

But only resembling. Now that she saw him at his best, she realised how far from ordinary he was. In the cell she'd been aware of brute force. Now she was even more intensely aware of the skill with which he disguised power. That made him a cunning man as well as a forceful one, and all the more dangerous for that.

It seemed odd to be regarding him as dangerous when his fate was in her hands, but he was no longer the down-and-out she'd met that morning. In fact, that had been an illusion. The reality was this other man who strode into the court as though he owned it, and took up position in the dock with an air of impatience, as though he were doing them all a favour.

She was his advocate, and obliged to do her best for him, but the temptation to bring him down a peg was almost irresistible.

The trial began. What happened then, Minnie could only ascribe to a malignant fate, making her life as difficult as possible. By dubious means Luke had contrived to wrap himself in a halo, at least as far as Netta was concerned. Now events conspired to give that halo a new brilliance.

The four oafs from the night before were also in the dock, grinning and scowling by turns. They had their own lawyer, ready to challenge Minnie on every point, and it soon became clear that they were trying to establish themselves as innocent victims.

They were all small and wiry compared to Luke's impressive size, and at one point their lawyer flung out a hand in his direction, inviting comparison. A sensible man would have let his shoulders sag, or at least done something, no matter how useless, to shrink himself.

Luke, to Minnie's total exasperation, stood up straight and folded his arms in an attitude that contrived to be aggressive. She could have torn her hair.

She redoubled her efforts, concentrated all her forces, managed to trip the oafs up, made them contradict themselves and showed them up for what they were.

Everyone relished the moment when the ringleader stumbled into silence while Minnie simply spread her hands as if to say, You see! The massed ranks of Pepinos began to applaud, and were firmly shushed by Netta.

More than a lawyer, Luke thought, unwillingly impressed. A consummate artist, a force of nature.

And he was going to be her next challenge. He was beginning to enjoy the prospect.

At last Fentoni declared that he was fed up with the lot of them, and imposed hefty fines all round.

One of the oafs, incensed at this 'injustice', made a lunging movement at Charlie, but found himself facing Luke, who stepped in quickly and took hold of his ear. While he twisted and yowled with pain Luke raised an eyebrow in the direction of the police, as though asking what he should do with this object. An officer hastily intervened. Fentoni promptly doubled the oaf's fine, and the session was over.

Netta beamed at Luke, then beamed some more when he insisted on paying Charlie's fine as well as his own. Charlie's brothers crowded round, slapping Luke on the back. Minnie groaned.

'Netta, he is not a hero,' she tried saying firmly. 'Charlie would probably never have been in trouble if he hadn't met him.'

'You've quite decided that I'm to blame,' Luke said, appearing beside her. 'Aren't you at least supposed to believe in your client?'

'You are not to blame,' Netta told him firmly. 'Tonight we have a big party at our home, and you will be the guest of honour.'

'You're too kind, *signora*,' Luke said impressively.

'You'll have no trouble finding the Residenza Gallini,' Minnie said darkly. 'You'll know it by all the bits falling off the building.'

'And if I don't notice them, I'm sure you'll point them out to me,' he said smoothly.

He was about to turn away when Minnie remembered something and stopped him. 'You need to call your mother,' she said in a low voice. 'She called you this morning while I was in your hotel room. I took a message.'

As she turned he stopped her with a hand on her arm. 'You will be there tonight, won't you?'

'Of course I will, if only to stop you deluding my poor family any more.'

His grin jeered at her. 'You haven't had much luck so far.'

'I'll improve with practice. Don't forget your mother,' she said in a voice that put an end to the conversation.

He took out his cellphone, which she had returned to him earlier, switched it on and dialled. Hope answered at once.

'Darling, I'm so sorry,' she said. 'I didn't mean to be indiscreet, but I forgot it was so early.'

'What do you mean?'

'This morning, when I called and the phone was picked up by that young lady. She sounded charming, but of course I got off the line at once.'

It dawned on him what she was talking about.

'No, Mamma, it's not like that.'

'Nonsense. When a young lady answers a man's phone at seven in the morning it's always ''like that''.'

He looked around and found Minnie's eyes on him. Of course she could guess every word his mother was saying. In outrage he turned his back on her.

'Mamma, listen to me—'

'Yes, my son,' she said and obligingly fell silent.

That stumped him. It had been the bane of his life that he had a mother who listened. Unlike other mothers, she didn't brush his explanations aside, thus giving him a permanent excuse—'But Mamma, I *tried* to tell you—' She simply sat there waiting, while he tied himself in knots.

Comparing notes with his brothers, he had found them all similarly afflicted. It had made growing up very hard. Now she was doing it again.

'You've got the wrong idea,' he growled.

'I hope not. I thought she sounded very nice. There was something in her voice, a soft vibration that's always there when a woman has a passionate nature.'

'*Mamma.*'

But then she surprised him with a great burst of laughter that rang down the line.

'Don't be silly, Luke, I'm only joking. She was probably the chamber maid bringing you an early breakfast. I expect you were in the shower.'

'Yes,' he said, filled with relief.

'It was wrong of me to tease you, but I would be pleased to think you were forgetting Olympia so soon.'

'Olympia?' he asked blankly. 'Oh, yes—Olympia.'

When he hung up a few minutes later he saw Minnie regarding him with a look he chose to interpret as cynical amusement.

'Do you mind telling me what you said to my mother?' he demanded.

'Very little. It was mostly of the "um—er" variety, and she needed no encouragement to think what you think she was thinking. She plainly believes that women clamour for a scrap of your attention and swoon with desolation if you don't look their way.'

He had been going to tell her that it was Hope's idea of a joke, but before he could do so she added, 'This was your first night in Rome and she reckoned you'd pulled already? Who are you? Casanova?'

'In my mother's estimation, yes.'

'Or did she think there was a simpler explanation, and that money came into it somewhere?'

'No, she knows I don't have to use money. At least, not in the sense you mean.'

'Is there another sense?' she demanded, aghast.

'I have been known to buy a lady dinner and the best champagne before a night of mutual pleasure. But nothing as crude as you're suggesting.'

Of course he wouldn't, Minnie thought before she could stop herself. This man would never have to pay a woman to get into his bed. The thought didn't improve her opinion of him. If anything, it added to his sins.

'I'm sure my mother never suggested any such thing,' he added.

'No she was very kind and assured me that she "quite understood perfectly". I suppressed the impulse to tell her that hell would freeze over first.'

'First?' he asked innocently. 'First before what?'

She regarded him icily. 'Before you wrap me round your little finger the way you've done with the others. Netta, *cara*.' She turned to embrace Netta who'd appeared beside her. 'I must be going to my office now.'

'Then you can give Signor Cayman a lift to the Contini,' Netta suggested quickly.

'I don't think—' Minnie began.

'But of course you can. It's just a little way past the Via Veneto.'

'The Via Veneto?' Luke queried.

'That's where my office is,' Minnie said. 'I'll give you a lift if you wish. Goodbye, Netta. I'll see you tonight.'

Luke didn't speak until they were on the road.

'I thought your office was in the Residenza. That was the address on your letters.'

'You might say I have two practices,' Minnie said. 'There's my official one in the Via Veneto, and my unofficial one here in Trastevere.'

'And the unofficial one is for friends, relatives—any of the locals likely to end up in a police cell?' he hazarded.

'I also act for my neighbours when they need help with a tyrannical, money-grubbing—'

'Meaning me?'

'No, meaning Renzo Tanzini. I fought him for ages

and then he—' She checked herself suddenly. 'This isn't the time.'

'No, this is where I thank you for helping me out. Send me your bill, and Charlie's, and I'll settle them promptly.'

'There's no need for that.'

'It's a good chance for me to get into Netta's good graces.'

'Surely you've managed that already?'

'And that makes you madder than anything, doesn't it? In your ideal world she'd hate me as much as you do.'

'I don't hate you, Signor Cayman, I merely require fair dealings for your tenants.'

'And you don't think you'll get them from me?'

'The tone of your letters didn't inspire hope.'

'The tone of *your* letters made me think of an elderly harpy with hobnailed boots.'

She gave a wicked chuckle that he found oddly pleasing. 'And I'll crush you, wait and see.'

He barely heard the words. Something in her voice had alerted him and, against his will, he found himself remembering Hope's words. '...*a soft vibration that's always there when a woman has a passionate nature...*'

Nonsense. Hope had invented it to tease him, and the power of auto-suggestion made him hear it now. Nevertheless, he found himself trying to provoke her into a response.

'I'm sure you'll try.'

'Oh, I'll do it,' she promised, 'but not just yet.'

Did he imagine it, or was there a special vibration in her tone as she said the last words?

They had reached the Via Veneto and were gliding along its length.

'Which office is yours?' he asked.

'Up there on the left.'

He studied it as they went past, and was impressed. He made the rest of the journey in thoughtful silence, breaking it only briefly when she dropped him at the hotel. She barely acknowledged his goodbye, speeding away in a dashing style that he couldn't help admiring.

His phone rang. It was Olympia, the girl he'd 'lost' a couple of days ago. It felt like a couple of years, so much had happened.

'Luke, are you all right?'

He stretched out on the bed. 'Of course I am. Don't worry about me.'

'It's just that you left so suddenly, and I didn't have a chance to say goodbye—and thank you.'

Her voice was sweet and husky, and now he remembered how it could entrance him. That, too, seemed to have slipped into the past a little.

'How's Primo?' he asked.

'As grateful to you as I am for bringing us together.'

'Don't start painting me as a noble loser,' he begged.

'A noble, generous loser.'

'Olympia, *please*!'

She laughed and it was charming, but his heart was safe. He hung up, feeling relaxed.

He stripped and went into the shower to scrub the police cell off. Now his thoughts were all of the coming battle, and how he should confront Signora Minerva. She had surprised him by being younger, prettier than his mental picture. Yet instinct told him that she was also more formidable and totally unpredictable.

Now he recalled something from early that morning. When Minnie had swept out of the cell on her way to his hotel, he and Charlie had been left to talk things over, and Charlie had said, 'Minnie and my brother Gianni adored each other. She hasn't been the same since he died.'

'She's a widow?' he'd said, surprised, for there was something about her air of glowing life that hadn't made him think of a widow.

'Has been for four years. And it's not for lack of offers. All the men are after her.' He'd sighed. 'Including me.'

'You're just a kid.'

'That's what she says. Not that it would make much difference if I weren't. I'm not Gianni. Gianni was everything. When he died, she died.'

It had meant little at the time, but now he tried to connect that picture with the vibrant, lovely woman he'd encountered since, and it was no use. It didn't fit. The surface denied the reality. Or maybe the other way around. How did a man tell?

Mentally he set that down on his plan of campaign. It could be very useful.

Even if he hadn't known where the Residenza was Luke would have spotted the party from a great distance. The courtyard was glowing, lights were on all over the building and more light poured out into the street.

He was reminded of the Villa Rinucci in Naples, his home for many years now, ever since Hope, his adoptive mother, had married Toni Rinucci. It stood high on a hill, and at night its lamps could be seen for miles inland and out to sea.

He had always loved the place. Even after he'd moved out to his own apartment in Naples, he'd looked up the hill at night before going to bed, and the sight had warmed his heart.

There was a wide gulf between the luxurious villa and

this down-at-heel tenement, and it was disconcerting to have the same feeling here as he found at home.

It was the lights, he told himself reasonably. Light always created the illusion of warmth and friendliness, and he wasn't going to start being sentimental about it.

But there was also the laughter and the sound of welcoming voices, and these, too, spoke of home, so that when he entered the Residenza he was smiling.

Behind him came the taxi driver, puffing under the weight of Luke's contribution to the party. When Netta called down to him from an upstairs window he indicated the cases of beer and wine. Cheers broke out above and the stairs shook under the pounding of feet. Several young men burst out into the courtyard, scooped up the cases and Luke with them. In moments he was upstairs, being embraced by Netta, who screamed joyfully in his ear, making him wince.

He'd met all the family briefly that morning, but now he met them again. Alessandro, Benito, Gasparo—all Charlie's brothers—plus Netta's brother Matteo, his wife Angelina and their five children. Netta's husband Tomaso slapped him on the back, hailing him as a saviour, and various other uncles and aunts clamoured for his attention, until he thought the little apartment would burst at the seams.

He couldn't see Minnie but in the crowded room it was hard to be sure, so he looked again, and then again. But there was no sign of her. He found himself curious to know how she would dress for this party.

Charlie bounded up to him, offering a drink.

'Thanks, but I'm sticking to orange juice,' he said. 'I'm not taking any risks tonight.'

'Go on, have a beer.'

'Don't press him, Charlie,' said a female voice. 'He doesn't want to end up burdened with you again.'

It was her. How long had she been standing there? When had she come in?

She was dressed with a flamboyance that surprised him. He'd never pictured her in trousers, but there they were, dark purple, fitting snugly over her hips, topped off with a silk blouse of extravagant pink. The effect was stunning.

Her fair hair was drawn back off her face, emphasising her delicate bone structure and fair skin, and she might have been a different person from the austere advocate of the morning.

'Thanks for coming to save me,' he said.

She laughed directly into his face. At five foot four inches she had to look up to him, but she still gave an impression of looking him in the eye, he realised.

'I reckon two doses of Charlie in one day is more than the strongest man should be asked to bear,' she said. 'Let me get you an orange juice.'

She fetched it, then had to turn to look after another guest. He watched her, unwillingly impressed by her neat, shapely figure. It was hard to reconcile this flaming creature with the woman Charlie had described, who'd died with her husband. There was something there he couldn't work out, something mysterious and intriguing.

The room was filling up as more guests arrived. Some of them gave him curious looks, and he guessed the news of his identity had gone around. He became lost in a maze of introductions. Every girl there wanted to flirt with him, and when someone put on some music there was dancing.

In such a small place it seemed impossible that anyone ~uld dance, but they managed it. Luke plunged in with ˙ sign of enjoyment, although he was actually growing tired after so long without sleep. But not for the world would he pass up the chance to win over his tenants, thus making them easier to deal with and, incidentally, giving himself the great pleasure of making Signora Minerva nervous.

At last he had a free moment just as Minnie was passing.

'You can't just go like that,' he said, grasping her hand. 'You and I have to dance with each other.'

'Have to?'

'Of course. When two countries are at war it's customary to mark a truce by having the two heads of state dance together.'

'I believe that only happens when the war's actually over.'

'Then we'll set a precedent,' he said, putting an arm about her waist.

Minnie might have demurred longer, but someone collided with her, pushing her closer to him.

'Very well,' she said. 'Just for the look of the thing.'

'You're all graciousness.'

Glancing up, she found him regarding her with a look that was half irony and half an invitation to share the joke. Drat him, she thought, for having a kind of fierce attractiveness that could get under her guard, even if just for a moment.

'How are you feeling now?' she asked.

'More human. A lot poorer.'

'You wait until you see my bill. That really will make you feel poor.'

'And Charlie's,' he reminded her.

'You don't think I'd charge Charlie, do you? He's my brother-in-law.'

He shook his head in despair for her.

'Why did you tell me that? You should have charged me over the odds for him and put the money into a fund for repairs.'

'Yes, I don't make much of a schemer, do I?' she agreed ruefully.

'You prefer to confront the foe full-on, rather than plot behind his back. Brave but foolhardy.'

'Plotting isn't my style. Besides, I've slain a good few foes in my time.'

'Is that a threat or a challenge?'

'Work it out.'

Minnie wished the room were a little less crowded so that she wasn't crushed so hard against his body. She'd seen that every woman in the place admired him, and there was something in that consciousness that infiltrated her own, so that she could understand their feelings, while assuring herself that she was safe from sharing them.

But she would have felt safer still if she could have danced a few inches away. The room was hotter than she'd realised, and it was getting harder to breathe.

As soon as she could she excused herself. 'I must go and help Netta. Enjoy the party.'

He nodded and let her go. He was beginning to be very conscious that he'd spent the previous night in a police cell, wide awake.

He'd meant to catch up on his sleep at the hotel that afternoon, but he'd become involved in business phone calls and in the end there had only been time for a cold shower. Now he knew it hadn't been enough. His eyes insisted on closing, no matter how hard he fought to keep them open.

At last, taking advantage of the crowd, he slipped out of the door and found himself by the railing that overlooked the courtyard. Too public. Where could he find a little privacy?

He discovered a small corridor that went through the building, connecting the staircase to the outer apartments that overlooked the road. It was deserted and he sank down to the ground, thankful for a place where a man could rest his head in peace.

He'd return to the party soon, but, just for a few minutes, he would close his eyes...a few minutes...a few...

CHAPTER FOUR

AFTER handing round more drinks, Minnie went into the kitchen to help Netta make coffee.

'You looked good together,' her mother-in-law observed.

'Just doing my duty,' Minnie said. 'It was purely formal.'

'How can you be formal with him? He is a *man*.'

'So are a lot of other people here,' Minnie observed, trying not to understand Netta's meaning.

'No, they are not men, like he is,' Netta insisted. 'Boys, feeble creatures who look like men but don't measure up. He is a *man*. He can bring you back to life. Why were you so careless as to let him leave?'

'Has he left?'

'Can you see him anywhere? He's slipped out with a woman, and they've found a quiet place to do things that—'

'Yes, I can imagine what they're doing.' Minnie stopped her hastily. 'I suppose he has every right to please himself.'

'He should be pleasing himself with you,' Netta said stubbornly. 'And you should be pleasing yourself with him.'

'Netta, I only met him today.'

'Huh! I only knew Tomaso one day before I had his clothes off. Oh, it was glorious! Of course he was useless at everything else but I got pregnant and we had to marry.'

'That sounds like an argument for staying a virgin.'

'Who wants to be dried up and withered?' Netta demanded.

Soon afterwards Minnie took the chance to slip away. Her nerves were jangling in an unfamiliar rhythm and she badly needed to calm them.

Taking up a bottle of mineral water, she went out of the front door, rejoicing in the cool night air. She took a long gulp of the water and felt better, then she began to drift down the stairs.

Perhaps Netta's right, she thought, *and I am dried up and withered. But I wasn't always…*

There had been a time when she and Gianni had seemed to exist for passion alone, a time when every night had been a scorching delight, every dawn a revelation, when life's chief good had been the shape of Gianni's body, the hot spicy scent of him.

But that time had ended. She'd told herself that his death had brought all desire to an end, and she was content to have it so. She was used to Netta's attempts to talk her into a different mood, and she'd always laughed them off. Suddenly, mysteriously, she couldn't do it any more.

Then she heard a noise from nearby. It came from one of the corridors that ran through the building, linking the inner staircase with the apartments that faced outwards.

Signor Cayman, she thought wryly, *taking his pleasures.*

But this didn't sound like a man in the throes of physical delight. More like snoring.

She crept inside the corridor. There was Luke, sitting on the floor, leaning against the wall, dead to the world. She dropped to her knees and, with the aid of one weak lamp in the ceiling, made out his face, slightly to one side, relaxed for the first time.

She'd seen his mouth tensed in the hard line of a man determined to have his own way, or twisted in derision, but now it was softened into a more attractive shape, one that it was just possible to associate with pleasure. Pleasure for himself, pleasure for the woman who kissed him...

She stopped, annoyed with herself for letting her thoughts wander in this direction. A woman who'd lived almost like a nun for four years should have herself under better control by now, except that somehow control grew harder as time passed.

It's Netta's fault, she thought, *talking about him and me like that.*

She was about to walk out and leave him, but her conscience stopped her. She couldn't let other people find him here. She gave him a gentle shake on the shoulder. It took several shakes before he opened his eyes.

'You've been sleeping like a baby,' she said, her eyes gleaming at him in the darkness.

'Oh, Lord, did anyone notice I was gone?' he groaned.

'Does it matter?'

'That place is full of young lads who can carouse all night and then start again without any sleep. At one time I could have done it, too, and I'm damned if I'll let them suspect I can't do it still.'

Minnie smiled and produced the bottle of mineral water, unscrewing it for him.

'Thanks.' He drank deeply and felt better. 'Whatever happened to my misspent youth?'

'You spent it,' she said sympathetically.

'Yes, I guess I did.'

'I wonder how. I'll bet you'd never seen the inside of a cell before last night.'

'There's no need to insult me,' he said drowsily. 'When I was younger I had my moments—I should be heading back to the hotel soon. I'll say goodbye to Netta and then—'

He tried to get up and sank back. His brief doze, far from refreshing him, had started dragging him down to the depths of sleep, and there would be no escape until he'd gone all the way to the bottom and surfaced gradually.

'You'll never make it,' she said. 'I've got a better idea. Stay here a moment.'

He fell asleep again as soon as she left, and awoke to the feel of her shaking him by the shoulder.

'Come on,' she said in a tone of command.

He had a vague awareness of going down a flight of stairs and along a corridor until they stopped outside a door. She took out the key that she had been to fetch, and opened the door of an empty apartment.

'This is between tenants at the moment,' she said. 'Of course you'll find it a bit of a comedown after the Contini—'

'If it's got a bed, it's fine,' he murmured.

'It's got a bed, but it's not made up.'

She reached into a cupboard to find a pillow that she tossed onto the bed, followed by some blankets.

'Hey, steady there,' she said, catching him swaying. 'Now lie down.'

'Thanks,' he mumbled, collapsing thankfully, and doing it so fast that she went down onto the bed with him.

'OK, let me go,' she said.

'Hmm?'

'Let me go.'

But the grip of his arms was unrelenting. He was too far out of it to heed her protests, but he was holding her against his chest in a grip she couldn't break.

She told herself that there was nothing lover-like about his clasp, and she must be as unaware of him as he presumably was of her. But the warmth of his great body was reaching her, enveloping her, taking control in a way that was alarming.

For a moment she was almost tempted. It was so long since she'd known the first moments of thrilling sensation with their implicit promise of what was to come, and it was hard to turn away now.

Yet she forced herself. Weakness was something she couldn't afford. That was the code she lived by, and she wasn't going to forget it now. Putting out all her strength, she managed to prop herself up a few inches, just far enough to deliver a well-aimed sock on his jaw.

Like magic he went limp, and she managed to get free.

'Sorry about that,' she said, untruthfully.

'Mmm?'

She tucked a blanket around him, and slipped quietly away.

At dawn Luke awoke and lay with his eyes still closed, trying to sort out his impressions. They were very confused.

A soft, warm, female body lying against his own—his head spinning—

He opened his eyes.

He was in a place he didn't recognise. The narrow bed beneath him stood in the corner of a small room which had a chest of drawers, a chair and a lamp. Nothing else.

He rose and pushed open the door leading to a living room with a small kitchen leading off. Like the bedroom it was sparsely furnished, containing only a sofa, two chairs and a table. The only other room was a small bathroom.

If only he could remember, but he'd been barely awake and had received only impressions. He'd held a woman close to his body and she'd been moving urgently—in the motions of love? Or trying to get away?

And who? Not the gazelle-like Olympia, who had sometimes filled his dreams, but someone shorter, more strongly built, with a powerful right hook he thought, as he recalled the reason his jaw was tender.

The sound of the front door made him turn. It was Signora Pepino, sauntering in and standing there, surveying him with a cheeky grin.

He barely recognised her. He'd seen her as 'Portia' in an elegant black gown, giving a commanding performance in the courtroom. Last night at the party she'd been glamorous in silk and velvet. Both of those women had been 'Signora Pepino'.

But this was 'Minnie', an urchin in old jeans and blue T-shirt. He wished she would stay the same woman for more than a few hours.

'So you're up at last,' she said with an air of teasing. 'This is the third time I've been back. You were dead to the world. Do you feel better?'

'Ye-es,' he said cautiously, making the word half a question, and feeling his jaw tenderly.

To his relief, she burst out laughing.

'I'm sorry about that.'

'It was you?'

She surveyed him with hilarity. 'Another woman would feel insulted by that question. Do women thump you so often that you can't remember them?'

'You're the first—I think.'

'Are we back to your misspent youth again? I'm not sure I want to know the details.'

'Fine, because I can't recall them.' He felt his jaw again. 'But I won't forget you in a hurry.' He looked around. 'Where did I see a bathroom?'

'No use. Everything's turned off. Come up to my place and I'll make you some breakfast.'

Now he could see the courtyard in broad daylight, and appreciate how cleverly the tenants had made the best of it. It might have been a dreary place with its dark bricks, plain construction and the staircase that ran around the inner wall looking like a fire escape. Indeed, it probably doubled as a fire escape, but it was also the way to get from one home to another.

But the dwellers here had fought back with flowers. There were several different kinds, but mostly geraniums, for Italians had a passion for geraniums, with their ability to spread colour and cheerfulness over the grimmest scene.

They were everywhere—white, red, purple, rioting over railings, trailing from pots, smothering ugliness. Just the sight of them lifted his spirits.

Minnie's apartment turned out to be opposite the one they'd left, but one floor higher. Whereas his had been a shoe box, barely big enough for one person, hers could manage two, three at a pinch, and had a cosy, friendly air.

She produced some towels and directed him to the bathroom.

'Breakfast will be ready when you've showered,' she said.

She hadn't quite finished cooking when he came out, and it gave him a chance to look around and see her home. Anything he could learn about her would be useful in the coming battle.

It was cosy and unpretentious, slightly shabby but delightful. He suddenly noticed a photograph standing on a shelf, with a small vase of flowers beside it. The man resembled Charlie, although he was older, and Luke realised this must be Gianni.

'That was my husband,' Minnie said, coming to stand beside him.

Gianni had a wide, laughing mouth, gleefully wicked eyes and the same air of irresponsible charm as Charlie.

'You can see that he's a Pepino,' Luke observed.

'Yes, they're a tribe of madmen,' she said with a slightly wistful smile. 'I love them all. He used to say that I'd have married any one of his brothers, just to be part of the family, but he knew he was special to me as no other man could be. Put it away, please.'

When he hesitated she took the picture from his hand and replaced it on the shelf.

'I'm sorry; I didn't mean to pry,' he said.

'You weren't. It's just that I find him hard to talk about.'

'After four years?'

'Yes, after four years. Sit down and have your breakfast.'

She was still smiling, still pleasant, but unmistakeably a door had been shut.

She served him eggs done to perfection and coffee that was hot, black and sweet. He was in heaven.

'I've seen people collapse at the end of a party before,' she said, sitting opposite him, 'but never from orange juice.'

'That's right, rub it in. At one time I could have seen that crowd under the table.'

'I doubt if you could ever have competed with Charlie,' she advised him.

'Was he really named after the Emperor Charlemagne?'

'Yes.'

'But why?'

'Because of Charlemagne's father. He was a king called Pepino.'

'And since the family name is Pepino—?' he hazarded.

'It stands to reason that they're descended from royalty.'

'But that was twelve hundred years ago.'

'So?' She shrugged. 'What's twelve hundred years to an ancient and royal family?'

'Do they really believe it?'

'Absolutely.'

'But surely it can't really be true?'

'Who cares as long as it makes them happy?'

'Isn't a lawyer supposed to care about the truth?'

'No, a lawyer cares about the facts. It's quite different. Anyway, that's for the courtroom. In real life a nice, satisfying fantasy is better.'

'You're like no lawyer I've ever known. You've got that office in the Via Veneto, which is the most expensive part of town, and yet you live here which is far from expensive. Perhaps I should double your rent.'

Her head jerked up. 'You *dare*—?'

'Calm down; I was only teasing. It seemed right to play up to your idea of me as Scrooge—sorry, Scrooge was an English villain—'

'You don't have to explain that to me. I'm half English.'

'You are?'

'My father was Italian, my mother was English. I was born here, and lived here until I was eight. Then my father died, my mother returned to England and I was raised there.'

Luke stared at her. 'That's incredible.'

'Unusual, maybe, but hardly incredible.'

'I mean that it's a sort of mirror image of my own experience. I'm completely English by birth. When my parents died I was adopted. But my adoptive parents divorced after a few years and my mother married an Italian called Toni Rinucci, from Naples. I've lived in Naples ever since.'

'So that's why you have an English name?'

'Yes. The Rinuccis are a family of English-Italian hybrids. Primo, my nearest adoptive brother, had an Italian mother, so he calls me *Inglese*, as an insult.'

She gave a gasp of delighted recognition. 'When Gianni and I were teasing each other he used to say, "Of course you're half English so you wouldn't understand," and I used to throw things at him.'

'Didn't you like being half English?'

She shook her head vigorously. 'I always wanted to think of myself as Italian. I got back here as soon as I could, and I knew at once that I'd come home, my real home. I met Gianni soon after, and we were married quickly. We had ten years. Then he died.'

She delivered the last few words briefly, and got up to make some more coffee. Luke said nothing, wondering at the sudden change that had come over her.

After a moment she returned, apparently cheerful again.

'So now you know why I live here. I love the whole family. Netta's a mother to me. Gianni's brothers became my brothers. I shall never leave.'

'But don't you ever feel the need to move on? I don't

just mean to another address, but emotionally, to the next stage in life?'

She frowned a little, as though wondering what the words meant.

'No,' she said at last. 'I was happy with Gianni. He was a wonderful man and we loved each other totally. Why would I want to move on from that? After total happiness, what is the "next stage"?'

'But it's over,' he said gently. 'It was over four years ago.'

She shook her head. 'No, it's not over just because he died. When two people have been so close, and loved each other so much, death doesn't end it. Gianni will be with me as long as I live. I can't see him, but he's still with me, here in this apartment. That's my "next stage".'

'But you're too young to settle for permanent widowhood,' he burst out.

'Who are you to say?' she demanded with a touch of anger. 'It's my decision. Gianni was faithful to me. What's wrong with me being faithful to him?'

'He's dead, that's what's wrong with it. Can't there be more than one man in the world?'

'Of course,' she said simply, 'but only if I want there to be.'

There was no more to say. She had closed the subject quietly but firmly. For a moment he glimpsed an iron will beneath the charming exterior. She would not be easily moved from a decision once taken.

'Thank you for breakfast,' he said. 'I'll be going now.'

'Let's fix an appointment so that we can go over this building and I can show you what needs to be done.'

'You've already given me a comprehensive list.'

'Yes, but the reality is worse. Shall we say tomorrow? I have a free afternoon.'

'I'm afraid I don't,' he said untruthfully. 'I'd like to arrange my own timetable. I'll call and speak to your secretary.'

Her wry look told him that she wasn't fooled. He met her eyes, letting her know that he wasn't going to be a pushover.

Before leaving he said, 'Can I have the key to the place where I slept last night? I'd like to look at it again. Thank you.'

The next few days were packed with work. The day she'd lost had to be made up and she had several new clients, so there was little time to reflect on the fact that Luke didn't contact her.

She took to going home late to avoid the curious looks of her fellow tenants. She knew they were excited at the prospect that she could really help them now, and they would be disappointed to know that matters had stalled. If Signor Cayman, as she persisted in thinking of him, did not call her, they would expect her to call him, and she didn't know how to explain that pigs would roost in trees first.

Nor could she have told them that one part of her was glad not to meet him again. When she thought of what she'd told him about Gianni and their lasting love, she was aghast at herself. She never discussed her husband with strangers, yet she'd found herself saying things to this man that she'd barely confided to Gianni's family. For some reason she cared that he should understand, but it made no sense, and it obscurely alarmed her.

Then a client suffered a crisis, forcing her to travel to Milan and stay for a week. During that time there was no call from him, according to her secretary. On the night before her return to Rome she decided that enough was enough, and called the Contini.

'I'm sorry, *signora*,' the receptionist said, 'but Signor Cayman checked out this morning.'

She flew back to Rome calling herself every name she could think of. He'd returned to Naples and her best chance was gone.

It was late but as she entered the courtyard Netta, followed by her menfolk, came hurrying to meet her, arms open.

'Darling, you're so clever,' Netta cried, enfolding her in a gigantic hug.

'No, I'm not. Netta, I've been stupid—'

'Don't be silly! You're a genius! Charlie, Benito, take her bags. Can't you see she's tired?'

Minnie found herself swept in and up the stairs.

'We've been longing for you to come home so that we could tell you how proud of you we are,' Netta said gleefully. 'It was a master stroke. You're simply a genius. Everyone says so.'

'Netta, will somebody please tell me what I've done that's so clever?'

'Oh, listen to her!' Netta chortled.

'But what—?'

Minnie fell silent as they reached the second floor. The door to the vacant apartment opened and a man emerged, regarding her satirically.

'What—are you doing here?' she asked slowly.

'I live here,' Luke informed her. 'I've just taken this apartment, although I have to say it's in shocking condition. First thing tomorrow I shall complain to the landlord.'

* * *

Meetings of the Residenza Tenants' Association always took place in Netta's home. This time the atmosphere was buzzing.

Netta dispensed coffee and cakes, besieged on all sides by neighbours who assumed that she was in the know. But what she could tell them was disappointingly thin.

'I've hardly seen her since she came home. She's been in her office early and late. There's been no chance to discuss anything.'

'But she must be talking to him privately,' was the consensus. 'Look at what he did today. She must have made him do it.'

But Netta said no more, unwilling to confide her suspicion that Minnie knew nothing about Signor Cayman's interesting activities that day.

At last the door opened and Minnie swept in, a mass of files under her arm, the picture of efficiency. To their disappointment, she was alone.

'All right, everyone,' she said crisply. 'We have a lot to talk about tonight. Things have changed, but we can turn this to our advantage—'

She stopped as the door opened, and her face showed her dismay.

'Sorry I'm late,' Luke said.

'What are you doing here?' The words were out before Minnie could stop them.

Luke's face assumed a look of diffidence. 'I thought this was the meeting of the Tenants' Association,' he said meekly. 'Did I come to the wrong place?'

He was drowned out by a chorus of welcome. Arms reached out to him. At first he seemed inclined to hold back, as if unsure, but then he let himself be drawn in.

And it was all an act, Minnie thought indignantly. If you believed this man was shy, you'd believe anything.

'Yes, this is the tenants' meeting,' she said, 'but I hardly think it's appropriate for you to be here.'

'But I'm a tenant,' he said, hurt. 'Haven't I the same rights as anyone else?'

She drew a long, careful breath. 'You are also the landlord—'

'Then I should be here, and you can tell me what you think of me,' he said with a winning smile.

'Signor Cayman, if you've been reading my letters you know very well what your tenants think of you.'

'But you were writing to me as landlord,' he pointed out. 'I'm here as a tenant, and I have several suggestions for dealing with the shady character who owns this building. I know his weaknesses, you see.' He added confidingly, 'There's nothing like inside information.'

This produced a ripple of laughter. Minnie had to respect these clever tactics, although she couldn't help feeling excluded. She was their friend and defender, yet he was taking over, make her superfluous. Suddenly she was shivering inside. It was a feeling she hadn't known since she'd returned to Italy, fourteen years earlier.

She knew what he was up to, pretending friendship only to turn on them later. But she wouldn't let him get away with it.

'You're quite right,' she said, giving him a cool smile to let him know that battle had commenced. 'But the really valuable inside information is held by me—information about this building and what it needs, what your tenants need. Without that, you know nothing. And if you really want to be well informed, *signore*, I suggest we start to inspect the building right now.'

That should show him that she had regained the initiative.

Then Enrico Talli spoke up.

'But Signor Cayman is already doing that. He inspected my place this morning, and Guiseppe's home this afternoon. He was most interested in what he saw, and has promised to take care of things.'

Minnie drew a long, slow breath.

'That is excellent news,' she said, hoping that her confusion and dismay weren't obvious.

'But what about me?' an elderly woman piped up, incensed that Enrico had received favoured treatment. 'When do you look at my place?'

'This is Signora Teresa Danto,' Minnie explained.

Luke smiled at the old lady. 'And what is wrong with your apartment, *signora*?'

'It's in the wrong place,' she said. 'I want you to move it.'

'That might be a little beyond my powers,' he admitted.

'It's on the top floor,' Minnie explained. 'And it's too large for her. Teresa needs something smaller and lower, so that she doesn't have to climb so many stairs.'

'Then perhaps I should take a look now,' Luke said, rising and offering Teresa his arm.

This brought a cheer from the assembled company, who all seemed to consider themselves invited. In a procession they left the room and followed Luke up the stairs to the top floor.

CHAPTER FIVE

TERESA'S flat was in reasonable condition, but too large for one person. As soon as they entered Luke's eyes were drawn to a low table on which stood a photograph of an elderly man.

'My husband, Antonio,' Teresa said with pride. 'This is where we lived together. Now he is gone, and this place is too big for Tiberius and me.'

Tiberius turned out to be an imposing black cat, sitting on a window sill, washing his face and observing proceedings with the indifference of one who knew that he would be all right, whoever else wasn't.

'Please move us on to a lower floor,' Teresa pleaded. 'I'm too old for those stairs, and Tiberius doesn't like heights.'

'In that case,' Luke said at once, 'you must take my flat, and I'll move into yours.'

There was a cheer of approval from the residents, and they all trooped downstairs to Luke's flat.

'We can start on the exchange tomorrow,' he said. 'It'll need redecorating—'

'Oh, no,' Teresa said quickly. 'It's lovely as it is.'

'It's not,' he said, surprised. 'It's a dump.'

'But redecorating will be expensive,' she said anxiously.

'Only to me, not to you. And, since it's so small, the rent will be lower than you're paying now.'

Teresa was ecstatic. 'Lower rent? Then Tiberius can have fish every day.'

'I guess he can,' Luke said, amused.

The old lady was as excited as a child who'd been promised a treat. She insisted that everyone must return to her home to celebrate and, since the tenants of the Residenza were always ready for a party, it was only a moment before the procession was making its way upstairs again.

Luke was the hero of the hour. Minnie, watching him cynically, could only wonder at the ease with which he was winning everyone over. His clever stunt with Teresa did nothing for the rest of them, but they didn't seem to notice that.

He made his way across the room to her. 'Aren't you pleased that I'm doing the right thing?'

'Never mind me. It's them I want you to please.'

'The truth is that hell will freeze over before you concede that I might have one good point.'

'Well—' she floundered.

Then she saw him looking at her with one eyebrow cocked and something on his face that might have been real humour.

'Maybe just one,' she conceded.

He grinned. 'That really had to be dragged out of you with pincers, didn't it?'

'Of course it did. I'm a dragon, remember?' She held out her hand. 'Goodnight.'

'You're not going?' he asked, scandalised.

'I ought to do some work—'

'Work won't do your headache any good,' he said shrewdly.

She stared. 'How do you know I have a headache?'

'Something in the way you keep closing your eyes. It's true, isn't it?'

'Yes, but it's just a little one.'

'It'll grow into a big one if you don't take care of it. No work. Come with me.'

'Why?'

'We're going to have a civilised coffee and a civilised talk, and celebrate our truce.'

'Haven't we already done that?'

As she spoke he was curving his arm around her, not touching her but shepherding her in the direction he wanted to go. She smiled and went with him, content to get out of the noise and glare.

Having urged her towards the stairs, he got in front of her.

'Just in case you fall,' he said. 'It's a long drop.'

'Hey, I won't fall apart because of a little headache,' she protested. 'I'm as tough as old boots.'

'Sure, I can see that by looking at you.'

As they went down, the noise faded behind them and she felt as though she were being engulfed by peace and quiet. It was a strange sensation to enjoy with Luke, but pleasant.

Coming out of the arch into the street, she took deep lungfuls of air, turning her face up to the sky with an expression of ecstasy.

'I suppose I look crazy,' she said when she opened her eyes to find him watching her.

'No, you look like someone who should do that more often. Feel better now?'

'Yes, it's a bit stuffy in that courtyard.'

They began to stroll through streets where *trattorias* were still open, their lights gleaming on the cobblestones. Luke saw an all-night pharmacy on the corner and slipped in for a moment.

'Just something for your head,' he told her, emerging, 'in case you find you're not as tough as you think.'

'Sometimes I'm not,' she agreed. 'Sometimes I just want to lie down and go to sleep.'

'You missed a trick there,' he said. 'Never admit a weakness to the other side. I shall pounce on it and use it to undermine you.'

She gave a rueful laugh. 'Will you?'

'Well, maybe not this time.'

'Besides, I already know your weakness.'

'I don't have one,' he said at once.

'You're a man who suffers badly if he doesn't get enough sleep. Look at the way you were after Netta's party. One night without sleep and you collapsed into a crumpled heap. You'll never take over the world like that.'

'I guess I won't. Dammit! What a pity you noticed.'

'Never mind. I won't tell anyone. I'll just "pounce on it and use it to undermine you".'

With every step Minnie felt she was walking deeper into calm content. The battle was far away. She would fight him tomorrow.

He steered her into a café where they could sit at a table on the pavement. The owner evidently recognised Minnie, for he held up a tall glass, raising his eyebrows in a question.

'What's that?' Luke asked.

'They do a delicious dish of strawberries, cream and ice cream. I used to eat it a lot before I moved to the Via Veneto and became pompous.'

He ordered coffee for them both and a sundae for her.

'Take this for your head,' he said, offering her what he'd bought in the pharmacy.

'Thanks. I'll leave it for a moment. It may not get bad enough for me.'

He watched with pleasure as she tucked into her sundae, thinking that it was like watching a child let out of school.

'They all lean on you, don't they?' he said suddenly.

'What?'

'The night we met, you came out to defend Charlie, and he's not the only one, is he? Rico let out a few interesting things while we were in the police station. You're in and out of that place, hauling them out of the consequences of their own mistakes. Shoplifting, low level smuggling, selling hot goods in the market—'

'It's all minor stuff. They're family.'

'They not *your* family. They've just latched on to you and loaded you with all their problems.'

'Why shouldn't they? I'm the strong one. I like it.'

'OK, you like it, but even the strong one needs a rest some times. Does anyone ever think of you?'

'Yes, Netta. She's been better than my own mother.'

But, even as she said it, she knew what he meant. On the surface Netta was the matriarch of the family, but in fact it was herself, and it was a lonely position.

She tried to remember the last time she'd walked through the streets of Trastevere like this, and she couldn't. It passed across her mind that under other circumstances Luke would have made an ideal friend.

Suddenly she realised that they were being watched. A young boy was standing on the edge of the circle of light, trying to attract their attention.

Luke noticed him and smiled. 'Hey there!'

As the boy came forward Minnie saw that he was holding a puppy.

'Is that—?'

'That's my friend,' Luke said. 'And *his* friend. So they're OK. Good.'

'I'm glad to see you well, *signore*,' the boy said with

formal politeness. 'I wanted to thank you for helping us the other night.'

'That's all right,' Luke assured him. 'It all ended happily.'

'But you were arrested—I know they must have fined you—and I have some pocket money—'

'There's no need for that,' Luke said. 'It's all sorted, and nothing for you to worry about.'

'You are sure?'

'Completely sure,' he said gently. 'But perhaps you shouldn't stay out so late another time.'

Right on cue a window opened somewhere above them and a woman's voice screeched, 'Giacomo, come home at once.'

'Yes, Mamma,' he called back in a resigned voice. He thrust the puppy towards Luke. 'He, too, would like to thank you.'

Luke rubbed the animal's head. There was another screech, and Giacomo hurried away.

'Why are you looking at me like that?' Luke asked.

'I guess I really did misjudge you. If there's one man in the world I wouldn't have thought—'

She was confused, less by discovering that there really had been a puppy, but by the kind way he'd spoken to the boy.

'It comes from having younger brothers,' he said, picking up her thought.

'Are you a mind-reader?' she asked in wonder.

'Well, it's easy with you, since I know where you're coming from. I'm the devil and all his works, and anything that doesn't fit that pattern takes you by surprise.'

She began to laugh and choked slightly, waving a hand before her face as if to fend him off while she got over it. He took hold of her hand and held it until she'd finished coughing.

'I suppose there'll come a day when we're not on opposing sides,' he mused. 'When that happens, there are things I'd like to discuss with you.'

It was hard to know how to answer him since his eyes were on her hand, not her face. But he didn't seem to expect an answer and, after holding her fingers between his for a moment, laid his cheek briefly against them and let them go. When she looked up he'd gone inside to pay the bill.

They walked on slowly. The moon was rising, making lovers draw back into the shadows, as she and Gianni had once done, she remembered. But there was no ache tonight, only a sense of peace that was almost happiness.

Even a group of lads kicking a football about down a side street couldn't disturb her. When the ball accidentally came flying in her direction she kicked it back with a neat movement that made Luke look at her with new respect.

'I can do more than stand up in a courtroom, you know,' she said, and they laughed together.

At last they came full circle to the Residenza and he saw her to her door.

'Have those pills before you go to bed,' he said.

But she shook her head.

'I don't need them now. I haven't had a headache for—I don't know. It slipped away without my noticing.'

'I'll say goodnight then.' He held her hand for a moment before turning away.

Back in his own home, he called Hope at the villa. When they'd discussed inconsequential things for a few minutes he said, 'I expect you see a lot of Olympia?'

'She and Primo were here tonight.'

'Next time, give her a message for me, would you?'

'*Caro*, is that wise? She and Primo love each other so much—'

'And I'm really glad they do. I wouldn't spoil it for the world. Mamma you told me once that everyone you love changes you in some way. So tell Olympia—just tell her I said thank you.'

Over the next few days the exchange took place. Luke had Teresa's furniture moved down for her, then he set about moving some furniture into his own place. This caused much hilarity among his tenants, as various items were hauled up five floors of stairs too narrow for them. The men turned out to help, and enjoy a laugh and a beer. The rest of the tenants came out to line the stairs, cheering and applauding as each item reached another level without doing anyone an injury.

After that it was Luke's turn to give a house-warming party. It was colourful and noisy and it competed with other Residenza parties as one of the best there had ever been. Minnie was working late, but she slipped in at the last minute to share a glass of wine and see how happy Teresa was.

'But I know you'll miss this place,' Minnie said, 'because it was the home you shared with Antonio.'

The old woman shook her head wisely. 'My home with Antonio is in here,' she said, pointing to her heart. 'And it will always be there. Bricks and mortar are nothing. You must be ready for what life offers you next.'

A stillness came over Minnie, and she had a strange sensation of hearing distant sounds from mysterious places, inaudible to anyone else but conveying a message to her. She turned away and saw Luke standing nearby.

It disturbed her that he might have witnessed that eerie moment.

'I'm sorry you couldn't arrive sooner,' he said.

'I tried, but I brought you a house-warming present. Here.'

It was a book about Trastevere, full of history and local colour. When he tried to thank her, she gave him a brief smile and slipped hurriedly away, running down the stairs to her own home, desperate to be alone. She locked the front door behind her, and stood for a moment with her back against it, as though barring the world. Teresa's words had got to her, and she could hear the distant music again.

She poured herself a glass of wine, took the photograph of Gianni from the shelf and curled up on the sofa, watching his face, waiting for the moment when he would become real.

She had done this many times before, and had devised a technique for making it happen. It was important to be patient. Trying to rush things would make it harder, so she let herself relax, holding the picture loosely in her lap, looking down on it with eyes that were vague and almost unfocused. Gradually the outlines of the room blurred, faded, retreated, leaving only him behind. And then he was there.

'I don't know what's the matter with me.' She sighed. 'Everything's in a muddle and I don't understand.'

He spoke in her mind. *Is it him?*

'Partly. He's playing a sort of game, but it's not a game to them.'

But if they benefit from it—?

'Will they? There's something going on here that I don't understand.'

Maybe it's really very simple, and Netta's right.

'No,' she said quickly.

Carissima, why are you angry?

'Because he's taking them away from me.' She sighed, facing the truth at last. 'My family, my friends, the people who looked to me—now they look to him. Since I lost you, they're all I have, and they're all I want.'

But suddenly there was silence. She waited for a long time, hoping for something more. But it was over.

Carissima, why are you angry? How often in their squabbles had he said that to her, gently teasing? She was the one with the temper, he the relaxed, good-natured one who waited until the storm had blown itself out.

Suddenly she felt very tired and lonely. She drew the picture up to her chest, folding her arms across it, hanging her head and thinking of Teresa, who could take Antonio with her wherever she went.

All about her the building was growing silent, lights going out. A couple remained on the outside staircase, but after a while even they moved away, unseen by anyone except Luke, who was looking out of his window, watching for the moment the staircase would be empty.

At last he slipped out of his front door and silently went down to Minnie's home. Watching her face, just before she'd left the party, he'd seen real hurt there, and it troubled him. He knew he was being unwise. Her power to make him feel protective was something he should fight, but he wasn't sure how.

One window of her living room looked out directly on to the staircase. The curtains were half open and he stopped to look in. The lights were low inside, but he could see her curled up on the sofa beside a small lamp. Then he realised that her lips were moving and her eyes were directed at Gianni's photograph, resting in her lap.

He drew in his breath and stood quite still, unwilling

to believe what he saw. But he had to believe it when she drew the picture up against her chest, her arms crossed over it as though clinging on for safety.

No, he thought despondently. Not clinging. Embracing. Because there was nobody else in the world that she wanted to embrace. She had found comfort, but not from himself.

He crept away. This was no place for him.

As part of furnishing his new home, Luke bought a couple of self-assembly bookshelves, which he set about putting together, soon realising that he had no gift for this. Trying to use a screwdriver, he slashed the back of his fingers, leaving him bleeding.

With no sticking plaster in the place, he was forced to wrap his hand in a handkerchief and go out to the pharmacy at the end of the street. As he emerged on to the staircase he saw a woman on the level below him, going down the last flight to the ground, then under the archway that led into the street. She was severely dressed in dark clothing and for a moment he was sure it was Minnie. He called down, but the woman didn't seem to hear him, and in another moment she had vanished.

He ran down the stairs and out into the street, but it was crowded and although thought he glimpsed her, he couldn't be sure. As he made his way down the street there was no sign of her.

In the pharmacy he bought a large packet of sticking plaster. On leaving he turned left down a small alley which would lead him to the Residenza by a back street. The little alley meandered for a while before emerging near the rear of a church. From here he could see the graveyard. It was a pleasant place, small and grassy, crowded with headstones that were warmed by the afternoon sun. While he stood watching, Minnie emerged from the church.

She was no longer alone. The other members of the family were with her, having probably come on ahead and met her in the church. They were walking in a little procession, led by Netta, with Minnie beside her and the Pepino brothers following. Luke stayed quite still, almost hidden among the trees.

They were all here together, dressed as mourners, which meant that this was a special day, Gianni's birthday or the anniversary of his death. He wondered what it meant to her after four years. Did she grieve for that charmer as a memory, or as a husband? Was he still alive for her?

Unwillingly he remembered the picture in her apartment, the way she'd embraced it as though it was the only comfort on earth. How often did she renew those flowers she kept beside it? How often could you renew love before it wore out?

They were drawing nearer, towards a grave that lay a little apart from the others. Netta was weeping as she approached it, and so were some of Gianni's brothers, but Luke was barely aware of their grief. His eyes were fixed on Minnie.

Alone among the family she was quiet. Her face was pale but composed as she knelt by her husband's grave. Then she rose and turned her attention to comforting Netta.

They were gathering around the grave now, loading it with flowers and talking to Gianni as though he were still one of them. From their smiles some of them seemed to be cracking jokes with him.

Luke knew he should move on, but something impelled him to stay a little longer and see this through to the finish. They were rising to their feet, moving slowly away.

Then, at the last minute, Minnie paused and turned for a last look, and Luke drew a sharp breath as he saw everything he would have liked to deny.

Her face was no longer composed but ravaged, desolate, anguished. All her life's joy was buried there, and Luke covered his eyes, suddenly unable to endure it.

When he raised his head again Minnie was looking directly at him with an expression of indignation and anger. He groaned. She would think he had been deliberately spying on her.

She turned away, contemptuously it seemed to Luke. He stood watching as the family disappeared into the church, then he hurried away, seeking to get back to the Residenza as fast as possible.

He needed time alone to think. Before his eyes she had changed into someone else. He'd known her, or thought he had, as sharp, funny, cool, in control. The other night he'd watched as she'd talked to Gianni's picture, but she'd done so with a gentle melancholy. The grieving, devastated woman of today was different, terrible.

Inside the flat he waited, listening, until night fell and the building was quiet. At last he descended the stairs to her apartment. The lights were on, but the curtains were closed. What was happening behind them? Had she taken shelter in her private world with Gianni, the world that excluded everyone else, especially him?

After a long time the curtains parted, revealing her face, but at once she let them fall.

'Minnie,' he cried, knocking on the door. 'Minnie, please open up. I must see you.'

There was no sound or movement, and he thought she

was going to ignore him. But then the door opened a few inches.

'Go away,' she said.

'I'll go when we've talked. Please let me in.'

Reluctantly she stepped back from the door. When he'd closed it behind him Luke stood looking at her. Their brief friendly intimacy of the other night might never have been. Now she was really his enemy, and for reasons that had nothing to do with the Residenza.

'I came to say I'm sorry,' he said.

'You were spying on me, and you think "sorry" covers it?' She spoke with her back to him.

'I wasn't spying. I'd been to a shop and happened to walk back that way. It was pure chance; please believe me.'

When she turned he was shocked by her face, which was pale and dreadful, as though she were living on the edge of endurance. 'All right, I believe you,' she said tiredly. 'But it's none of your business, and I don't want to talk about it.'

'Do you ever talk about it, with anyone?'

She shrugged. 'Netta sometimes—no, not really.'

'Don't you think you should?' he asked gently.

'Why?' she asked wildly. 'Why can't I have some privacy? Gianni and I—this is mine. It's *mine*. Can't you understand that? It's between Gianni and me.'

'Except that there is no Gianni,' he said, suddenly harsh. 'He's just a memory now. Or maybe no more than a fantasy.'

'What does that matter? He made me happy then and he makes me happy now. Not many people ever have that kind of happiness. I want to keep it.'

'But you can't keep it. It's gone, but you'll turn your back on life rather than admit it.'

'Who cares about life if I've got something better?'

'There *is* nothing better.'

'People who say that don't know. They don't know what it's like to be so close to someone that it's as though you were one person. Once you've had it, you always have it. You *can't* let it go. Why should you try to make me?'

He'd been asking himself that, and the answer scared him.

'Can't you see that you're too young to live with a ghost?' he said, almost imploring.

'The only thing I can see is that you have no right to interfere in my life. What I do or don't do has nothing to do with you.'

'You can't prevent me wanting to stop you throwing your life away.'

'It's mine, to do with as I please,' she said, angry and frustrated that he wouldn't understand. She paused, took a deep breath and spoke with an effort. 'Look, I'm sure you're a nice man—'

'Be honest. That's not what you really think of me.'

'All right, No! I think you're a smug, patronising, interfering, arrogant so-and-so, who's playing games with my mind for the fun of it. I don't like you. You're too damned sure of yourself. Is that honest enough for you?'

'It'll do for starters.'

'Then please go and leave me alone.'

'Why? So that you can have another chat with a man who isn't there?' he demanded harshly. 'Which of you dislikes me most? Him or you?'

'Both of us.'

'Do you do everything he tells you?' he shouted.

'*Get out!*'

He hadn't meant to say his last words but her stub-

bornness was causing something cruel and dangerous to
rise in him, and it made him leave, fast, shutting the door
sharply behind him. Outside, he stood on the staircase for
a moment before going slowly down to the ground and
out of the courtyard, to spend the rest of the night wandering the streets of Trastevere in a black mood.

CHAPTER SIX

THE next day he received a call from her secretary, making a formal appointment in her office. He wore a respectable suit in dark grey, with a snowy white shirt and a dark red tie, and was glad of it when he saw her office, a large, impressive room, the walls lined with legal books.

Almost as if inspired by the same thought, Minnie too wore a grey suit with a white blouse. He briefly considered making a mild joke about their similarity, but a glance at her face changed his mind. She was pale, with very little make-up. Her hair was drawn back against her skull in a way that seemed designed to deny life—or, perhaps, to send him a message.

'There was no need for that, you know,' he said gently.

'I'm not sure of your meaning.'

'Aren't you? I thought you might understand. Oh, well, never mind.'

'Signor Cayman, if we keep to the matter in hand I think we'll make more progress.'

Her voice was cool, self-possessed, the voice of a woman in control of the situation. But he heard in it something else, a tension that made him look at her more closely, and realise that her eyes were dark and haunted.

'I'm sorry,' he said suddenly.

He hadn't meant to speak the words, but they burst out.

'There's no need for apologies,' she replied coolly, 'if we can just stick to business.'

'I didn't mean that. I meant I'm sorry for the things I said the other night. I had no right—it was none of my business—'

'Excuse me,' she said swiftly, and left the room before he could realise what she meant to do.

He frowned, hardly able to believe that she'd fled him, unable to cope with what he was saying. How deep a nerve had he touched with his rash words?

The secretary brought him coffee. He drank it, then passed the next few minutes standing at the huge window, looking out over Rome. From here the view was breathtaking, with its distant view of the dome of St Peter's, glowing under the sun. If he hadn't known it before he would have known now that Signora Pepino was a supremely successful lawyer who could afford everything of the best. It gave a new poignancy to her refusal to leave her shabby old home.

Minnie appeared ten minutes later, her composure restored.

'I apologise for that,' she said. 'I remembered a phone call I had to make.'

She seated herself, indicating for him to take the chair facing her desk. 'I gather you've now been over the building extensively and seen for yourself what needs to be done.'

'I have,' he said, sitting down and opening his briefcase, 'although we may not have the same ideas as to what needs to be done.'

'You've seen the state the place is in?'

'Yes, and I don't think repairs are any more than sticking plaster. What that building needs is to be renovated from top to bottom. It's not just a case of flaking plaster, but rotten woodwork needing to be ripped out and replaced.'

'Your tenants will be very glad.'

'Minnie—'

'I think *signora* would be more appropriate,' she interrupted, looking not at him but at the computer screen.

His temper began to rise. If she wanted to play tough, OK. Fine!

'Very well, *signora*, let me make my position plain. My tenants are paying about half the going rate for property in that area, which is perhaps why my predecessor got into financial difficulties.'

'Trastevere isn't the wealthy part of Rome—'

'It's coming up in the world. I've researched the area, and I know that Trastevere has been growing more popular over the last few years. People who couldn't afford the high prices in the rest of Rome started moving in and doing the place up. So then Trastevere prices started to rise. It's actually becoming fashionable to live there.'

'I see where this is leading. You've had an offer from a developer and you're planning to sell us out. Forget it. Your predecessor tried that, but I stopped him by proving that the tenants are protected. They can't be got out for at least ten years. That scares the developers off, except that some try bullying tactics. But even they can be made to wish they hadn't started anything, as you'll find out if you tangle with me.'

'Can I get a word in edgeways?' Luke snapped. 'Whatever needs to be done at the Residenza I want to do it myself, and I want the rest of you to help me. As for bullying tactics—if that's what you think of me, I don't know why we're even bothering to talk. To hell with you for thinking such things!'

He threw down his papers and strode across to the window, staring at the view without seeing it. All he could see was the turmoil in his own mind, where she had the power to cause such havoc. Her opinion of him shouldn't matter, yet her contempt seemed to shrivel him.

'I apologise,' she said, behind him. 'I shouldn't have spoken so strongly. I don't like being taken by surprise, and you surprise me all the time. So I—I go on to the attack.'

'I really am sorry about the other day,' he risked saying. 'I didn't mean to spy. It was an accident.'

'I know. It's just that there are times when I don't like to be looked at.'

'I think that's most of the time,' he suggested gently.

'Well—never mind that.'

'But I—damn!'

The telephone had rung. She snatched it up and spoke to her secretary, finishing with, 'All right, put him through.'

She made a placating signal to Luke and spoke into the phone for ten minutes.

When she'd finished he asked, 'Could you block your calls until we've finished?'

'Not really. I have some important stuff coming through this morning—'

'And it gives you a convenient escape from me, right?'

Before she could answer, the phone rang again. Moving fast, Luke lifted the receiver and slammed it back down. Then he grasped Minnie's hand and began to walk out of the room, forcing her to go with him.

'What do you think you're doing?' she seethed, trying to pull free.

'Taking you to where there's no escape,' he said, not loosening his grip.

On the way through the outer office they passed the secretary, whose curious gaze forced Minnie to look cheerful.

'Just take messages until I'm back,' she called.

'But when will that be?'

'I have no idea,' she managed to say before the door closed behind her.

'What kind of man are you?' she demanded as they went down in the lift.

'A man with a short fuse, a man who doesn't like being messed about, a man who believes in direct action.'

'So your answer is to take me prisoner? Where are you going to put me? In a dungeon?'

'Wait and see.'

But he grinned as he said it and there was something in the sight that sent a sudden *frisson* through her. It was confusing not to know what he had in mind, but also strangely intriguing. His unpredictability should be maddening—it *was* maddening, she hastily corrected herself. But right now she was intensely curious.

After all, it might actually turn out to be a dungeon.

The ride to the 'dungeon' was by one of the horse-drawn carriages that travelled the streets of Rome.

'Borghese Gardens, the lake,' Luke called to the driver as they got in and seated themselves.

'You're going to throw me in?' she asked.

'Don't tempt me,' he growled.

She decided to wait and see before taking any hasty action. Not that there was much action she could have taken with her hand firmly clasped in his.

New York had Central Park, London had Hyde Park, Rome had the glorious Borghese Gardens, known as the 'green lung' of the city, a hundred and fifty acres of trees, lawns, shaded wandering paths and cool water.

At the top of the Via Veneto the driver turned his horse into the gardens, and soon they were trotting beneath trees through which the sun slanted, until the lake burst on them, its water glistening, the artificial temple on the other side white and gleaming in the glow of summer.

Leaving the carriage, Luke led her to the place where boats could be hired, but suddenly a tremor shook her and she tried to pull away from him.

'Not here, Luke.'

'Yes, here,' he said firmly, keeping tight hold on her hand. 'We're going to take a boat and relax and talk and forget everything except that it's a beautiful day.'

'But—'

'Hush,' he said, raising the hand that was holding hers so that she could see the tight clasp as well as feel it. 'I told you there was no escape and I meant it. Today, *Signora Avvocato*, you're going to do as you're told— for once.'

Not releasing her, he took a small rowing boat, and indicated with his head for her to get in. She did so, and he silently congratulated himself. Evidently the odd display of 'male authority' could be risked, even in this day and age.

She settled in the stern, watching him as he took the oars and headed out into the middle of the lake.

'You were right,' she mused. 'There's no escape.'

He had a mysterious feeling that she meant something else, but she fell silent.

'Do you mind?' he asked cautiously. 'I'm sorry I got pushy.'

So much for male authority, he thought.

'It doesn't matter,' she said, and again he had the sensation that she wasn't really talking to him. 'It had to happen. I suppose I was being silly.'

'I seem to see a new you all the time,' he observed. 'In party mood, mother hen, the stern lawyer today—'

'You've seen me as a lawyer before,' she reminded him. 'Think of our first meeting.'

'That was different. That court was your stage. You commanded it. But I haven't seen you before like you are today, holding yourself in and fighting the world. Or is it only me?'

'No,' she said after a moment. 'As you say—the world.'

'You do a lot of fighting inside yourself, that nobody knows about, don't you?'

She nodded.

'Or perhaps Gianni knows?'

He knew it was a risk but, instead of trying to jump out of the boat, she shook her head.

'Did he ever know?'

'When he was alive there was nothing to fight,' she said simply.

He pulled on the oars, drawing them nearer the centre of the lake, sensing that the further they went the more she relaxed, as though a spring inside her was visibly uncoiling.

'*Signora*—' he began.

'Minnie.'

'Then could you please take your hair down? It's scaring me.'

She laughed and pulled her hair free, letting it fall around her face, as close to dishevelled as he had ever seen it.

'Is that better?' she asked.

'Much better,' he agreed. 'Now you look like the real Minnie.'

'You know nothing about Minnie,' she assured him.

'True, because she keeps changing and confusing me.'

'I could say the same about you. You've had a few

different guises yourself—convict, party animal, ruthless tycoon. I merely adapt to keep up with you.'

'And what am I now?'

'Caveman! Hauling me off like that to a place where there's no escape.'

'Well, there *is* no escape, unless you want to jump into the water. I don't know if it's deep but it's certainly dirty.'

For answer she gave the most delightful chuckle he'd ever heard from her. It subsided into a sweet, wistful smile.

'What is it?' he asked.

'How strange that you should have said that to me. It's exactly what he said.'

'He?' Luke asked, but he had an uneasy feeling that he already knew the answer.

'Gianni. This is where he proposed to me. He hired a boat just like this one, rowed me out into the middle of the lake, and said, "Marry me!"'

She fell silent, looking into the water, reliving the moment.

Luke stared, shocked as the implications dawned on him. Then he groaned and clutched his head with one hand, so agitated that he forgot the oar, which swung away from him in the rowlock. Minnie leaned forward to take hold of it.

'Don't panic,' she said, sliding it back to him.

He didn't seem to see it. He was staring at her, aghast.

'That was why you didn't want to come on the lake?'

'Yes.'

'This place is special, and I forced you... Oh, Lord, I'm sorry. I shouldn't have done that. What a mess!'

'Stop being so hard on yourself.'

'Have I ruined it for you?'

'Of course not,' she said gently. 'Nothing could ruin it for me. It doesn't depend on other people. I'm even glad that you made me come here. I've never been back since he died, and it's been like a wall rearing up in front of me. Now you've helped me get over it.'

Her air of strain had fallen away, leaving her calm and content. She had said, 'It doesn't depend on other people', and he saw that it was true. She had her own world where she lived with Gianni, and nobody could touch it.

Luke cursed the ill luck that had made him bring her here. He'd meant to draw her away from Gianni's ghost, but it was himself from whom she'd withdrawn, back into her private place, leaving him outside.

He took the oar from her, feeling the brief touch of her hand. Slight as it was, it unnerved him.

He said no more for a while, but rowed in silence while the sun rose high in the sky and he grew uncomfortably hot in his sedate jacket.

'You're not dressed for rowing,' she said kindly. 'Why not take your jacket off?'

He removed it gratefully and she took it from him, folding it neatly and laying it beside her.

'And the tie,' she said. 'Take that off and open your shirt. Right now you need to be comfortable rather than dignified.'

'Thanks,' he said, stripping off the tie and handing it to her.

It was bliss to open the top buttons and feel the air on him, but after a few minutes he discovered a downside to this. Perspiration cascaded from him as he rowed, soaking his shirt, making it cling to him, outlining the muscular shape of his torso.

For some reason he felt awkward. With any other beautiful woman he would have enjoyed the chance to impress her as part of the normal process of flirtation. But for her that wasn't good enough, and he felt uncomfortable, even ashamed.

He glanced at her and was relieved to find that she apparently hadn't noticed. She was leaning back, her head tilted up to the sky. Her eyes were closed against the sun, and there was a half smile on her lips. He watched her, entranced, knowing that he could have stayed like this for ever.

He pulled on the oars with renewed vigour, relishing the mass of physical sensations that were rushing in on him at once. Exertion had made his blood pound and his heart beat more strongly, and now his memory seized on the night of the party, when he'd fallen asleep, she'd led him to bed and had to struggle to free herself.

He couldn't actually recall her thumping him, but the feel of her body writhing against his was there with him now. And suddenly he knew why. The touch of her hand, a few minutes ago, had revived that other moment when they had been as close as lovers, in flesh if not in spirit.

Now his body felt alive, vibrant, and the knowledge that it wasn't the same with her, that there was no way he could reach her, had the effect of intensifying every feeling almost to the point of desperation.

In an urgent attempt to distract his own thoughts, he said, 'Did you accept Gianni at once?'

'I didn't say anything,' she remembered dreamily. 'I was too dumbfounded to speak. I was madly in love, but I'd thought it would take me ages to wring a proposal out of him. Suddenly there it was, and all I could do was open and close my mouth like a goldfish.'

'What did he say?' Luke pressed her.

He despised himself for weakening and asking the question, but if she didn't tell him soon he'd go crazy.

'He said, "Either you say yes or I tip you in the water." So I said yes. Afterwards he told me he wished he hadn't done it that way, as he'd never know whether I'd married him out of love or to save myself from getting wet.' She laughed. 'I told him to work it out.'

'Did he ever manage that?'

'Let's just say we were very happy,' she said softly.

He was silent. There was nothing to say.

After a moment she asked, 'Why are you looking at me like that?'

'I was wondering how often this happens. Do you see Gianni everywhere?'

She considered this seriously. 'I don't "see" him. He's just there, part of me.'

'But I meant places.'

'Yes, he's in all the places. Anywhere we were together, he's still there. We often used to come on this lake and remember what happened.'

He was longing to ask if Gianni was there with them now, but he bit the words back. Why torment himself?

'I should return to the office,' she said with a little sigh.

'Let's not go back. Let's stay on the water, then go and have some lunch and to blazes with them all.'

'I can't,' she said reluctantly. 'I have clients coming in this afternoon.'

'Put them off.'

'Luke, I can't. I mustn't. I can't just abandon people who need my help.'

'But we haven't talked about anything.'

'Serves you right for being a caveman.'

And with that he knew he would have to be satisfied. Turning the boat he pulled back to shore and helped her out. A horse-drawn carriage was passing and took them back to the Via Veneto.

At the door of the building she paused. 'We'll talk business another day,' she said.

Luke didn't want to talk business with her. He wanted to kiss her. But he bade her a polite farewell and left.

A few minutes walking in the sun were enough to dry his shirt. He called the bank and made himself an appointment for later that day. He passed the time with an excellent lunch at which he drank only mineral water to keep his head clear. By now he was functioning as a businessman, so he sat at the table for another hour, jotting down figures.

The meeting at the bank was very satisfactory, and he emerged with the feeling of having matters under his control, something which always made him feel better.

But he was restless, and to ease it he walked all the way back to the Residenza while the light of the city faded and the yellow lamps came on. It was almost dark when he arrived.

Some of his neighbours were sitting on the stairs of the courtyard and he lingered with them, exchanging pleasantries. But he didn't stay long. It had been a hot day and a humid evening, and he was longing for a shower. As he climbed the final stairs he allowed himself to glance down at Minnie's windows, something he hadn't allowed himself to do under the curious eyes of his neighbours. There were lights on. She was in.

Briefly he considered crossing over to see her, but he sensed that she would prefer to be left in peace. After watching the lights in her flat for a while he closed his door and went into the bathroom. There he stripped off, got under the shower and reached out to the boiler.

It exploded.

*   *   *

After that his impressions piled in on each other. The hideous noise, the crack on his head as he was hurled back against the wall, flames, the terrible helplessness of lying on the floor, half in and half out of consciousness, unable to move and save himself.

From a distance he heard fists pounding on his front door until it flew open and people burst in. Some dragged him out of the bathroom, others fought the flames. The pain was terrible, yet he didn't lose consciousness, only turned his head from side to side, trying to understand what was happening.

They wanted to carry him outside where he would be safer, and he thought vaguely that they shouldn't do that because he was naked. He tried to say something, but when he looked up he found Minnie's face above him. Somehow she was cradling him in her arms. Tears poured down her face and she was sobbing, 'Oh, God, not again—*not again*!'

Then he blacked out and knew no more until he awoke to find himself in hospital. There was a searing pain down his right side, starting with his face, which felt red-hot, and going down his arm, where it was almost unbearable. He made a sound which was half gasp, half groan, and a woman's face appeared in his consciousness.

'You're awake. Good. The pain-killers should start to take effect soon.'

Luke gave a grunt of thankfulness.

'What happened?' he whispered.

'Your boiler blew when you were right in front of it and you caught the full blast. You're lucky you aren't dead.'

'I feel pretty near it.'

'Your right side is most affected. You have mild burns

The Harlequin Reader Service® — Here's how it works:

If offer card is missing write to: Harlequin Reader Service, 3010 Walden Ave., P.O. Box 1867, Buffalo NY 14240-1867

BUSINESS REPLY MAIL
FIRST-CLASS MAIL   PERMIT NO. 717-003   BUFFALO, NY

POSTAGE WILL BE PAID BY ADDRESSEE

HARLEQUIN READER SERVICE
3010 WALDEN AVE
PO BOX 1867
BUFFALO NY 14240-9952

NO POSTAGE
NECESSARY
IF MAILED
IN THE
UNITED STATES

all down the right of your body, and more severe ones on your arm. But they'll heal. You're in no danger.'

He remembered now. He'd just stripped off, prior to having a shower when the world had exploded about him. With horror he realised that the woman talking to him was a nun.

'Oh, Lord!' he groaned. 'I'm sorry, sister—'

'Doctor,' she said firmly.

'Doctor, I hope I didn't outrage the sensibilities of the sisters.'

'Don't you worry, young man,' she said cheerfully. 'We're not easily scared. Besides, you were decently covered by the time you came in. Your neighbours took care of that.'

'Good,' he said thankfully.

But then more memories assailed him. Minnie—she'd been there when they'd dragged him free. He'd lain naked in her arms, and she'd cradled him, weeping, 'Oh, God, not again!'

He tried to think. Had it really happened or was it just his feverish imagination? But the pain-killers were taking effect and suddenly he lost consciousness.

CHAPTER SEVEN

HE SURFACED again, having lost track of time, but seeing that it was still dark outside. Turning his head painfully, he saw Minnie standing at the window with her back to him. He tried to speak but the sound that came out was weak, and she didn't turn towards him. He wished he could see her reflection in the dark glass, but her head was bent.

Minnie, standing at the window, knew that he had stirred, but needed a pause before she could look at him. She kept her head lowered, lest he see her face, and her tears should reveal too much.

She could still hear the explosion. It happened again and again in her head until she thought she would go crazy from the endless repetition. Then everything slowed and she seemed to be wading through glue as she ran to him, her heart pounding at the sight of the smoke and flames.

It was playing back again, the moment she'd rushed in to find them dragging him out of the bathroom and laying him out on the floor, dropping to her knees beside him, cradling him in her arms—like that other time—watching life ebbing away—*Please, not again!*

She'd held him against her, willing him to live, begging, praying, imploring some unseen power, because she couldn't bear to go through it a second time.

They had taken him from her arms to get him down the stairs. She'd followed and insisted on going in the ambulance with him.

Now he was safe, his injuries treated, his outlook good. She ought to be glad and relax, but inwardly she was screaming while the tears poured down her face.

'Minnie.' His voice was barely a croak, but her ears seemed specially sensitive to him, and now she couldn't hide any longer. She dried her eyes and forced herself under control. When she turned to him she even managed a smile.

Through a haze Luke watched her come towards him and lean close.

'You're all smudgy,' he whispered.

She rubbed her face. 'It's the smoke.'

'Sorry about that. Were you injured?'

'Not at all. Never mind me,' she said with soft urgency. 'I'll go soon and let you rest, but first, how do I contact your family?'

'There's no need for that. I'd rather not worry my mother. She'll think it's worse than it is.'

'You were lucky it wasn't.'

'I was lucky in my neighbours, who came to my rescue so fast. Still,' he added wryly, 'I suppose, having won me over, they wanted to keep me alive until the repairs were done.'

'Stop fishing for compliments. You're a popular man.'

'But you can't think why.'

At one time she would have enjoyed bantering with him, but now there seemed to be a lump in her throat and she was afraid of weeping again.

'I haven't given the matter any thought,' she said, trying to speak steadily. 'Now, can we please be serious for a moment? I ought to let someone know about this. What about your girlfriend?'

'What girlfriend?'

'The one whose picture you keep in your wallet. I

found it the first night when I was collecting your things. She has lovely long black hair.'

'Oh, her!'

'Oh, her? Is that any way to talk about the lady in your life?'

'Hardly that.'

She was silent for a moment before she spoke, choosing her words carefully. 'Does she know she's been relegated to "Oh, her!"?'

'Olympia wouldn't care. To her I was never any more than "Oh, him!"'

'Yet you kept her picture.'

'I'd forgotten it was there. Better tear it up now she's engaged to my brother Primo. In fact—I don't know—what was I going to say?' His mind seemed to be filled with clouds.

'Never mind now,' she said. 'Get some rest. I'll come in tomorrow.'

'Thank you for—what you did—it was you holding me, wasn't it? Or did I imagine that?'

'Go to sleep,' she said.

'Mmm!'

She waited and, when she was sure that he was asleep she kissed his forehead. He stirred, but did not awaken, and she slipped out silently.

The next day he felt better, although still woozy. Netta came to see him, bearing a huge gift of fruit, and chattered non-stop.

'Everyone asked after you. Benito and Gasparo and Matteo, and they sent you some beer, but the hospital wouldn't let us give it to you.'

'They're funny about that,' Luke said with a weak grin.

'Such a mess you were, we thought you would die. So

we called the ambulance and when they carried you off we followed. All except Minnie. She came with you.'

Did she cradle me, naked, in her arms? he thought.

'I'm glad I've got such nice neighbours,' he said.

Netta continued bawling kindly confidences at him until a sister came to his rescue and ushered her out.

'Thanks,' Luke said when the sister returned. 'She's a dear, but—' He gave an expressive shrug, then wished he hadn't because it hurt his arm.

'No more visitors today,' she said.

'Ah—well, if Signora Minerva Pepino should come, I want to see her. She's my lawyer and we're planning legal action against my landlord.'

He slept again and when he awoke it was dark outside and Minnie was sitting beside him. Her dishevelled, grimy look was gone and she was her impeccably neat self again.

'Are you feeling better?' she asked.

He was still talking in a husky whisper, but he managed to say, 'Yes, I guess I'm well enough for you to say, "I told you so."'

She smiled faintly. 'I was going to save that for later.'

'Go on, get it over with. Aren't you glad that I ended up my own victim? Doesn't it serve me right? Minnie, what's the matter?' She'd covered her eyes suddenly and when she spoke her voice shook.

'Don't say things like that, just—don't.'

'You're not crying, are you?' he asked in disbelief.

'No, of course I'm not,' she said hastily, brushing her eyes. 'But you could have died in that blast.'

'Teresa *would* have died in it,' he said huskily. 'She's old and the shock alone would probably have finished her off. I'd have had that on my conscience.'

'Then she's very lucky that you took over,' Minnie

said gently. 'We all are. Thank God you're still alive and it's no worse than a burned arm and face.'

He gave a derisive grunt. 'That's no loss. Women never pursued me for my beauty. I might do better as "scarred and interesting".'

'You're not going to be scarred. Here.'

She took out a small mirror and gave it to him. He surveyed himself critically and grunted again.

'My face looks like a boiled lobster.'

'Only down one side,' she reassured him.

He gave a bark of laughter and immediately winced.

'Just a little redness,' she said. 'It'll go and your looks will be unimpaired.'

He looked at her askance. 'My face was always shaped for scowling rather than smiling. Now it feels too tender to smile much, anyway. Tell me about the apartment.'

'Blackened with smoke. The fire was put out almost at once, but it's not habitable.'

'I want you to do something for me—I mean, please. Get the right people in, not just to my place but everywhere. I want every boiler in the building replaced, and that's just for starters. When I'm back home there's a lot more to be done. I want to oversee it personally.'

'You need to be better before you can think about anything.'

'Will you come and see me again?'

'Of course.'

The nun he'd spoken to earlier appeared by his bed, and smiled at the sight of Minnie.

'*Signora*, I am glad to see you. Signor Cayman tells me that you are both planning to take very stern action against the landlord.'

Minnie's lips twitched. 'He said that?'

'Oh, yes, and it's good. Such landlords are beneath

contempt. If I had yours here I would put arsenic in his coffee.'

'So would I,' Luke said, darting a wicked glance at Minnie.

'You're looking tired,' she said. 'It's time I was going.'

She gave his hand a brief squeeze and departed, leaving him to the tender mercies of the sister.

In three days he was feeling better. He still lacked energy but the only sign of injury was his heavily bandaged arm and hand.

The Pepino family visited every day. Netta would call in briefly to ask if she could get him anything, and the men lingered to play cards.

'Netta, I want to get out of here,' he said one evening. 'Is my place really so bad?'

'You can't live there,' she said at once. 'Not for ages.'

'What about a hotel? Do you know one nearby?'

'You can't live in a hotel. You come to us.'

'I couldn't impose on you. There would be so much work—'

Netta began to weep noisily. In the outpouring that followed several things were stressed—her lonely life since so many of her sons had moved out, how happy it made her to have someone to look after, but, of course, at her age she couldn't expect to know the joy of being needed, and if he preferred to go among strangers then she would try not to complain, but it was very hard on a poor woman who only wished him well, et cetera, et cetera.

Her sons listened to this with groans that showed they'd heard it all before, and her husband leaned over to Luke, remarking cynically, 'You may as well give in now.'

Luke agreed and yielded, grinning. Netta's tears dried as if by magic, and she graciously accepted the financial terms he offered. It was agreed that he would be collected the next day.

Minnie arrived soon after, to be greeted by the news. She expressed herself pleased, but there was a slight reserve in her manner that Luke thought he understood.

Even so, he might have been surprised to hear them talking in Netta's kitchen that night.

'What are you playing at?' Minnie demanded furiously. 'And don't give me that innocent look because you're as devious as an eel.'

'Bad girl. You should respect your mother-in-law.'

'I'll respect her when she stops trying to marry me off.'

'Marry? Who says marry? I'm looking after an invalid, that's all.'

'That's all, my left foot! This is part of a devious plan.'

'So? I'm your Mamma, you've said so often. And a Mamma is supposed to be devious to help her daughter.'

'I do not need help,' Minnie declared, trying to sound firm.

But she knew, from experience, that it was easier to be firm with the wind than with Netta in full cry.

'Of course you need help,' Netta said. 'Four years you are a faithful widow. Now you find a happy life for yourself.'

Minnie eyed her with wry affection. 'So this is all about my happiness, is it?' she challenged.

Netta shrugged expressively. 'He's rich. You marry him, we won't have to pay rent ever again.'

'Netta, you don't know what you're playing with. This

isn't a game where you can move people around the board like pawns. I—I don't want him here. I think he should stay in hospital a little longer.'

'If he's here he's in your power and that's what you want.'

'Really? So now you're an expert in what I want?'

'Sure. You want a man.'

'Not this man,' Minnie said stubbornly.

'Yes, this man. He's the one. I, *your Mamma*, tell you so.'

'Will you keep your voice down?' Minnie asked frantically.

'Then be a good girl and do as you're told. You want him here where you can work on him, like any clever woman.'

'Well, maybe I'm not a clever woman.'

'That's true. You're a very clever lawyer, *cara*, but a stupid woman.'

'Thanks,' Minnie said crossly.

'Don't sulk,' Netta advised her. 'Mamma knows best.'

'She's right,' Tomaso said, looking into the kitchen. 'You listen to Netta. She's got it all worked out.'

'You should be ashamed of yourselves, the lot of you,' Minnie said, but she spoke without anger.

Their affection warmed her even while she told herself that they were scoundrels conniving for their own benefit. That was true, but it wasn't the whole truth. Their schemes were survival ploys, and their love for her was genuine. So, as often before, she allowed herself to be seduced by the comfort of their embrace. The fact that she disapproved of them did not make that embrace one whit less comforting.

She was in court the following day and so missed seeing Luke's triumphant return to the Residenza. Coming home late, she saw Netta's lights on, and Charlie keeping watch on the stairs to waylay her.

'She's here,' she heard him call inside.

They swarmed out to engulf her and sweep her inside, where Luke rose to greet her. He was smiling and composed but she sensed an air of strain. When Netta ordered her to sit down and eat, Luke insisted on bringing some of her supper from the kitchen and helping to serve her.

'You look as if you should be in bed,' she told him quietly as he poured her coffee.

'I'm a bit tired, but Netta's looking after me wonderfully, and they're making me feel like one of the family.'

'That's what I'm afraid of,' she said softly. 'They're lovely people, but—'

'But exhausting. I know. Don't worry. Netta says she's going to be like a mother to me. Tomorrow I have strict orders to stay in bed until the nurse comes to change my dressing. Then I'll get up and go up to look at what's left of my home.'

'Don't overdo it. You need all your energy for getting well. Is your room comfortable?'

'Yes, I've got Charlie's room. He's kindly moved into a tiny place that looks like a box cupboard.'

'It would have been better if you'd had that one.'

'Thanks,' he said, surprised.

'No, I mean it's down the end of the corridor and fairly quiet. Charlie's room is in the centre, and always noisy.'

'Well, it's still kind of them, and I won't be here for long.'

Before she left, Minnie took Netta aside.

'He looks very tired,' she said.

Netta sighed and nodded. 'Perhaps this wasn't a good idea. With so many of the family around and the others dropping in, he can't rest properly.' Suddenly she brightened and seemed to think of something. 'I know, why don't you put him in your spare room?'

Minnie groaned. 'This is what you've been planning all the time, isn't it? Netta, you are unspeakable, you are shameless, you are—ooh, I wish I could think of something bad enough.'

'I know,' Netta said penitently. 'I'm very bad. But you will take him, won't you?'

'I will not. I refuse to be a party to your schemes, do you hear? I don't know how you have the nerve to—of all the—*Goodnight!*'

She grabbed her bag and got out of the apartment while she could still control herself, leaving Netta to explain to Luke that there had been an urgent call from a client.

Minnie meant to stay away for the next few days, but the memory of Luke's strained face haunted her.

Part of her wanted to take him in, care for him and enjoy doing so. But part of her shied away. Being honest, she didn't hide from the reason. It was connected to the minutes when he'd lain in her arms, burned, bleeding, helpless.

His nakedness had left no doubt of what she'd often suspected, that he was magnificently built with broad shoulders and strong thighs, designed for power. Suddenly the power had gone, leaving him vulnerable, his eyes closed, his head slumped against her. The desire to protect him at all costs had been overpowering, and that was what she feared now—to be overpowered, not by him, but by the strength of her own feelings.

She'd stroked back his hair, caressed his face and shoulders, held him against her heart, weeping frantically. And for a few blinding minutes she'd cared for nothing and nobody else on earth.

Now, despite her resolve to stay away from danger, she knew he wasn't well, and she had an uneasy feeling that she'd abandoned him when he needed her. So she called the following evening, meaning to stay just a few minutes.

She found the place in uproar and Netta weeping.

'I meant everything to be all right,' she wailed, 'and now everything is all wrong, and I don't know what to do.'

'But what's happened?'

'My sister Euphrania and her husband Alberto are on their way here to visit us. They will arrive tomorrow and expect to stay here but we have no room. Oh, what am I going to do?'

Suppressing a desire to murmur, 'Stop overacting,' Minnie drew Netta firmly aside.

'This is another of your schemes,' she said, 'but it isn't going to work. He's not coming to my place.'

Netta gave her a pathetic look. 'What will become of him?'

'You'll have to pass on to Plan C, won't you?'

'Pardon?'

'Yesterday was Plan A and it didn't work, this is Plan B, and it's not working either.'

Netta's eyes gleamed. 'The day isn't over, *cara*.'

'Your day will be over for good if you don't stop this,' Minnie threatened. 'I won't have him at any price.'

Netta giggled. The sound infuriated Minnie.

'I will not invite him, Netta. Understand me once and for all, the answer is *no*!' She added, more in hope than conviction, 'And that is final!'

She stormed away so fast that she collided with Luke coming along the corridor, and he winced before he could stop himself. In the brief harsh close-up view of his face, she saw that he was at the end of his tether.

'I'm sorry,' she said. 'I didn't mean to hurt you.'

'I'm fine,' he lied. 'Minnie, is there a good hotel near here?'

She hesitated, seeing a malign fate draw closer, ready to suck her in, and there was no way to avoid it without kicking him when he was down.

'Not a hotel,' she said. 'Not among strangers.'

'I'm a grown man. I can take care of myself. Netta, there you are. I was just wondering about a hotel.'

'I don't think that's a good idea,' Minnie said reluctantly.

'But of course it is,' Netta cried, to her astonishment. She named a hotel. 'It's a lovely place. You'll be very comfortable there.'

'He will not,' Minnie said hotly. 'It's a dump run by swindlers.'

Netta became an avenging angel. 'The night porter is my cousin's uncle's brother.'

'I rest my case. Swindlers who fleece the guests and provide bad food. Luke could die in his room and not be discovered for days. No way. He'll stay with me.'

'I wouldn't dream of troubling you,' Luke said at once.

'It's no trouble,' she snapped.

'Then why did you say earlier that you wouldn't take him at any price?' Netta demanded.

In the icy silence that followed, Luke looked from one to the other.

'Did you say that?' he asked, sounding only mildly interested.

'I—may have said something like it, but I've changed my mind. I don't want your fate on my conscience, so you're coming to stay with me.'

'Don't I get a say?'

'No. And that's final.'

'You say "final" very often,' Netta mused. 'Only then things turn out not to be final at all.'

'Netta, I'm warning you—' She checked herself and drew a long, slow breath. 'Please be kind enough to collect Luke's things.'

'Suppose I say no,' Luke said. 'Perhaps I don't want to.'

She turned on him, breathing fire. 'Did I ask what you want? You are coming to stay with me, and that's the end of it. No more argument.'

'You'd better do what she says,' Netta told him. 'When she's made up her mind, she never changes it. Never, *never* does she change her mind—'

Then, perceiving that she had pushed her beloved daughter-in-law as far as was safe, she fell silent.

'Then I guess I'll just have to agree,' Luke said with an air of meekness that did nothing to improve Minnie's temper.

She glanced at the other woman, expecting to see her relish her triumph. But Netta had left the field of battle while she was winning.

The whole family helped him move the short distance to Minnie's flat, where Netta got to work on his bed.

'Come and see if it's all right,' she commanded Luke, guiding him, not to the spare room, but the large bedroom with the double bed.

'I'm taking the spare room,' Minnie told him. 'Netta says you toss and turn a lot, so you'll be more comfortable with the extra space.'

'I can't take your room.'

'It's all arranged,' she said. 'So quit arguing.'

He didn't want to argue. He didn't want to do anything

except collapse on the double bed, which looked wonderfully inviting. Minnie, reading his face, shooed everyone out so that he could have some peace. The last one to leave was Netta, and Minnie went with her to the door.

'You're disgraceful,' Minnie told her amiably. 'There was no need to hurry it tonight.'

'Best if neither of you had time to change your mind.'

'It won't work, Netta. Luke and I just aren't on that wavelength.'

'Hmph! Much you know! Goodnight, *cara*.'

Minnie laughed and kissed her. 'Goodnight.'

She closed the door and went back to the bedroom where she had left Luke. But he was already sprawled across the bed, fast asleep.

CHAPTER EIGHT

LUKE settled into a peaceful routine in which he slept a lot, had his dressings changed by the visiting nurse, and entertained visitors.

Teresa came every day with Tiberius. If Luke had been her hero before, he was doubly so now that he had received injuries that would otherwise have descended on herself and possibly the cat.

'The dear old girl has somehow persuaded herself that it was all a plot against Tiberius's life,' he told Minnie one evening, 'and that I charged in at the last moment, seized him up and put myself between him and the blast.'

'What was Tiberius doing taking a shower?'

'He's a cat of many talents, according to Teresa.'

'And nobody will ever make her understand the truth,' Minnie said ruefully. 'That, but for pure chance, you'd have been the villain and I'd have been suing you, on Teresa's behalf, for every penny you have.'

He grinned. 'Better luck next time.'

They had fallen easily into this way of talking, still opponents, but teasing each other almost like brother and sister. In the mornings she would rise first and bring him coffee. When she'd left he'd embark on the awkward business of washing himself with only his left hand, and the nurse would help him finish dressing.

After that there would be a procession of Pepinos and various other neighbours, bearing food and entertainment. The afternoons became a card school, with Luke insisting on small stakes and being careful to lose.

Minnie would return when the evening was half over, looking tired and with a briefcase full of files. Once he tried to prepare a meal for her and made such a clumsy mess of it that she asked pointedly if he were trying to destroy her home as well as his own.

It was Netta who did the real cooking, sweeping in every evening with an elaborate meal that she swore she'd 'just thrown together', then sweeping out and not returning until the next morning, which surprised him. Such restraint was unlike Netta.

After supper Minnie would settle down to work while he watched television. He'd offered to turn it off but she assured him this wasn't necessary, as her concentration was deep enough to blot out distractions. And it was true, he realised, regarding her bright head bent over the papers. Her private world was always there, the door open invitingly.

He only wished he knew who was waiting for her in there. It hadn't escaped his attention that she'd removed Gianni's picture from his sight.

One evening Minnie put her books away, then yawned and stretched. From behind the half-open bedroom door she could hear Luke talking into his phone, and heard him say, 'Mamma.'

As he hung up she pushed the door right open. 'Cocoa?'

'Lovely.'

He came out and settled on the sofa until she returned with two mugs.

'Have you told your mother what happened to you?' she asked.

'Not yet. I'll tell her when I'm human again.'

'Tell me some more about your family. How many are there?'

'Eight, including our parents.'

'Six brothers and sisters?'

'Just brothers. Hope, my adoptive mother, had a son when she was fifteen and obviously unmarried. Her parents gave him up for adoption and told her he was dead.'

'Swine,' Minnie said succinctly.

'I agree. None of us knew anything about him for years. Hope married Jack Cayman, a widower with a son called Primo, because his mother had been Italian. And they adopted me. I don't think it was ever a very happy marriage, and it collapsed when Franco, Primo's uncle, came visiting from Italy, and he and my mother fell in love and had a son.

'After the divorce she got custody of me, and Primo stayed with his father, but Jack died a couple of years later and the Rinuccis took Primo to Italy. Hope went to look for him, and that was how she met Toni, Franco's brother, and married him.'

'What about Franco? If she had his baby, didn't she go to him after the divorce?'

'No, he already was married with two children, and he felt he couldn't leave his wife.'

'Doesn't that make family reunions a little tense?'

'They don't happen often. Franco lives in Milan, which is a safe distance.'

Minnie was counting on her fingers. 'So how do you get six sons?'

'Toni and Hope had twins, Carlo and Ruggiero. And then last year the first son, Justin, turned up, and there was a big reunion. He came to Naples to be married—'

Luke's voice trailed off as he realised something that astonished him.

'What is it?' Minnie asked, looking at him more closely.

'He married barely six weeks ago,' he said, sounding dazed.

'Is that odd?'

'I left the next day, so it means that I've only been here for six weeks.'

So much had happened that he seemed to have known her for ever, yet it was all crowded into that short space of time. He knew it was true, and yet he couldn't believe it.

'Just six weeks,' he murmured, looking at her.

She met his eyes and he knew that she had understood. Suddenly the truth was there between them, undeniable, even for her. He reached forward to touch her face with gentle fingers.

'Minnie—' It was no more than a whisper.

'Luke—please—please—go on telling me about your family.'

The moment was over, so fleeting that it had barely happened, and even he, the least subtle of men, knew that to try to prolong it would be to court disaster.

'Yes,' he said. 'Well—we're an odd family, some related, some sort of related, some not related at all.'

'But the only one not at all related is you,' she said shrewdly. 'You're a Cayman in the middle of a family of Rinuccis. Don't you feel left out?'

He considered this.

'I'm not sure. Justin isn't a Rinucci either. He's Justin Dane.'

'And Primo, presumably, is a Cayman too.'

'No, he took the family name years ago. I could have done the same. Dear old Toni said he considered me as much his son as his own boys, and I was welcome to be a Rinucci if I wanted.'

'But you didn't want to?' she asked, sounding puzzled.

'Do you think that's strange?'

'I can't understand anyone choosing not to be part of a family if they had the chance. It's so—so cold outside.'

'I'm not exactly outside, or only to the extent that I choose to be. I guess there's just something pigheaded in me, something that makes me stay outside the tent, or at least to be free to leave when I want. Does it matter?'

'I suppose it might matter to the people who tried to welcome you, and maybe were left feeling rejected.'

'I think they understood.'

'Of course they understood, if they loved you, but that doesn't mean they weren't hurt.'

He frowned, but before she could speak she checked herself.

'I shouldn't have said that, please forget it. It's your business. I love being part of a large family, and I forget that some people feel suffocated by it.'

'No, not suffocated,' he said quickly. 'It's just that— you're right. I'm the only one that isn't related by blood to any of them. I'd never really thought of that before, yet I suppose, in a way, it's always been at the back of my mind that they all belong together in a way that I don't.'

'But that's meaningless,' she said earnestly. 'I'm not related by blood to the Pepinos, but I'm still one of them, because they want it and I want it.'

They said no more, but her words stayed with him, keeping him awake long into the night. There was, in her, an open-hearted acceptance of life, and a need to seek and embrace warmth, that he knew to be lacking in himself. And he had never been so conscious of it as now.

The work he'd ordered was getting under way. Engineers had surveyed the building, identified several other boilers that they considered dangerous, but passed most of them as safe.

'It doesn't matter,' Luke told Minnie as he folded up the papers one night. 'I want them all replaced. Every one. And stop giving me that cynical look.'

'I'm *feeling* cynical. You're playing the hero again, the grand gesture—'

'Give me patience!' he roared. 'Woman, will you stop thinking the worst of me at every excuse?'

'I don't need an excuse, and don't call me woman.'

'What would you prefer? The creature from the black lagoon?' he asked, reminding her of their first meeting in the cell.

'No, that's my line,' she said, laughing, for these days their battles had lost the hostile edge and were more like humorous fencing.

'Anyway, it's nothing to do with playing the hero. It's Netta. Her boiler doesn't need replacing, but if you think I'm going to face her with *that* when Signora Fellini next door is having a new one, you can think again.'

'Coward!' she said amiably.

'Sure I'm a coward. Netta scares me—not as much as you do, but enough.'

'Oh, yes, you're very scared of me! Who do you think you're fooling?'

She'd been cooking and was now sitting beside him on the sofa, her face flushed from the heat of the kitchen, and prettier than he had ever seen it. Suddenly all his good resolutions deserted him, and he reached out, cupping his left hand behind her head and drawing her face close to his.

'If I weren't terrified of you, you harpy, I'd kiss you right now.'

'But you are terrified of me,' she reminded him in a voice that wasn't quite steady.

You could take that two ways, he thought: as a rejection, or a dare. He was always up for a dare.

Moving clumsily, he managed to get his bad right arm around her as well.

At this distance Minnie couldn't miss the disturbing smile on his lips, and an even more disturbing look in his eyes.

'I'm getting braver by the moment,' he said. 'Still nervous of your right hook, though.'

'No need for that,' she murmured. 'I wouldn't fight an injured man. It wouldn't be—correct.'

'That's right,' he said, lowering his lips. 'I might sue.'

In the four years of her widowhood she'd had light flirtations, short-lived relationships that had died almost before they lived. A kiss and it was over, dying in disappointment and despair.

But Luke's kiss was different, shocking in its intensity. Briefly Minnie put up a hand to protest, but then let it fall away. Sensations that she'd banished from her life were threatening to take control of her. They were purely physical, unmixed with tenderness, but thrilling, driving caution out.

It was crazy, reckless to kiss him back, but she found herself doing it, using both arms to clasp him, one hand seizing his head in a mirror image of his own movement, so that she could press her mouth more closely to his.

Now there was no going back, even if she'd wanted to, but there was nothing she wanted less. All the sensuality she'd suppressed was rising up to torment her, crying out that there was life still to be lived. The skills she'd thought she'd never need again clamoured for use, reminding her of how sweet it was to be held in a man's arms, especially a man like this, who knew how to use his lips to tease a woman until she melted.

She opened her mouth a little, teasing him back, inviting, while her hands explored him, relishing the shape of his head, his shoulders. Every movement was a violation of the rules she lived by but she didn't care. There would be time later for regrets—but there would be no regrets—regrets—

Suddenly the word shrieked at her out of the darkness. She lived with a secret that caused her such bitter regret that there was almost no room in her life for anything else. She'd survived on caution, and she was throwing it recklessly away.

She must escape the trap her own madness had created for her, and there was one way, one weapon calculated to drive him off.

Fighting the pounding of her heart until she could control herself, Minnie pressed her hands against Luke's chest, just enough to let him know that she meant it. He drew back a little, regarding her with eyes that held a question, and a hope.

'This is a bad idea,' she said.

'Minnie—' His voice was urgent.

'You really are a very brave man,' she said, hoping she didn't sound breathless and trying for a light humorous tone.

He regarded her, still with the same disturbing gleam that made it so hard for her to laugh.

'Why, are you going to thump me after all?' he murmured, giving her a quizzical look that almost sent her back into his arms.

'Much worse than that,' she said. She drew right away from him, leaning back on the sofa and regarding him humorously. 'Luke, you're such a clever man, I'm amazed that you didn't see through it.'

'See through what?'

'Netta's cunning little plan. Do you think it was an accident that her relatives suddenly announced a visit when you were there?'

'It seemed a bit odd, especially as there's been no sign of them.'

'Of course not. That visit was conveniently cancelled as soon as Netta achieved her object, which was to get you down here, with me. Luke, wise up! Don't you see what she's trying to do?'

'You mean—you and me?'

'She's trying to marry us off.'

'She's what?'

'Netta is setting up a match between us. If she can bully us up the aisle, all the Residenza problems are solved—she *thinks*. I've tried to make her understand that she's got it all wrong, that there's no way you and I would ever think of getting married. But as fast as I fended off one plan she came up with another.'

'She's trying to—?'

'She's an arch conspirator. Don't worry, I have no designs on you. I only brought you here because you looked so wretchedly ill that I couldn't leave you to her mercies, but you're quite safe. What happened just now—well, it didn't mean anything.'

His eyes kindled. 'Didn't it?'

'Hey, it's been four years. How long can a woman live like a nun? You're an attractive man. OK, I was tempted. Haven't you ever been tempted even while one part of your mind was saying, Better not?'

'Oh, yes,' he said ironically. 'That just about describes

my state of mind since the day we met. You've had "better not" written all over you, but I like risks.'

'So you took one, and it was nice, but now we've both come to our senses—'

'Have we?' he asked raggedly.

'Well, unless you want to be marched up the aisle at the point of Netta's shotgun—' A thought seemed to occur to her. 'Oh, Luke, I'm sorry. Are you saying you *want* to marry me? I never thought—'

'Of course not,' he said quickly. 'That is—I don't mean to be rude but—'

'Neither do I, *but!*' she broke in quickly. 'That's the whole point, isn't it? *But!* Two people kiss and it doesn't mean anything. Let's keep it that way. I just hope—'

With a convincing air of sudden alarm she dashed to the window to check the curtains.

'Lucky they were drawn,' she said. 'Nobody can have looked in. Just a moment—'

She made a play of opening the front door and looking out on to the staircase.

'Nobody there,' she said, returning and locking the door. 'We've got away with it. Our secret is safe.'

She turned out her hands with a bright air, as if saying, You see?

'Well, thank goodness for that,' Luke said, rallying and matching her apparent mood. 'Thanks for warning me.'

Hell would freeze over before he let her suspect how far he felt from laughing.

After that they were both glad to bring the evening to an end. They smiled and assured each other that it was all a good joke, and escaped each other as soon as possible.

Luke sat up for a long time, brooding in the darkness, wondering if his pain-killers were to blame for what was happening. They were strong, and he sometimes felt that they caused his thoughts to go astray. What else could account for the sudden blazing moment of illumination that had come on him with the discovery of Netta's plan?

He didn't want to laugh. He wanted to say that Netta was the wisest woman in the world. He wanted to seize Minnie's hand and jump into the deep end with her at once.

But, as a sensible man, he would resist this craziness, and hope that a night's sleep would return him to normal.

When Netta learned that she was to have a new boiler the upshot was predictable. Overjoyed, she immediately announced a party.

'Why not wait until the boiler's installed?' Minnie asked.

'Silly girl, we'll have another party then,' Netta chided her.

'Of course, I should have thought of that.'

'Yes, you should,' Luke agreed. 'Even I could see that coming.'

Netta drew Minnie out on to the staircase, well out of earshot, to ask, 'How is everything going?'

'It isn't,' Minnie said, adding defiantly, 'we're like brother and sister.'

Netta was horrified. 'He hasn't—?'

'No, he hasn't.'

'Then you're not trying hard enough,' Netta declared, and departed in high dudgeon.

Minnie didn't immediately return inside. To have told Netta the truth would have been impossible. She was no green girl but a woman who'd experienced years of passionate love. Yet that one kiss had left her thunderstruck.

It might have been the first kiss of her life, so disorientated had it make her feel.

Everything about Luke that antagonised her at other times—his power, his determination and masculine forcefulness—had been transmuted into fierce excitement the moment his lips had touched hers. It was like dealing with two men, one who could drive her to a passion of anger and opposition, and one who could thrill her to the depths, making her yearn to become one with him.

But they weren't two men. They were one. And the confusion was driving her crazy.

In desperation she'd revealed Netta's plan so that they could laugh about it together. It had partly worked, but it did nothing to help the feelings that coursed through her at the thought of him, especially at night.

Darkness had fallen. All over the courtyard, lights glowed out of the windows on to the geraniums, illuminating flashes of colour. Looking up, she saw the building winding upward until it seemed to reach a disc of sky where stars wheeled and circled before vanishing into infinity.

How often, after Gianni's death, had she looked wistfully at that infinity? Now it merely seemed cold and bleak, and she hurried back inside to where Luke was waiting, maddening and impossible, but somehow comforting.

The party was the following evening, and the first hour went as she had expected, with Luke being hailed as everyone's saviour. He grinned at her.

'Try not to look as though you've swallowed a hedgehog,' he murmured.

'Don't be so unfair. You've earned this, and I don't grudge you a moment of your popularity.'

'Liar,' he murmured in her ear, his warm breath sending shivers down her neck.

But soon after this she began to realise that something was wrong with him. His mouth had grown tense and his forehead was wet. Moving quietly, she slid beside him, firmly dislodging the young female who was flirting with him.

'Time to go home,' she murmured.

'Nonsense, I'm fine.'

'You're not fine, you're in pain. And like a good mother hen I'm going to take you home.'

He nodded and didn't try to argue any more. Minnie said a word to Netta, then guided him firmly out of the room and down the stairs to home.

'You know what they're saying back there now, don't you?' he asked with grim humour.

'After seeing us leave early, you mean?'

'Yes. Netta will expect an announcement tomorrow. What will you say to her?'

'Nothing, I'll just smile enigmatically. It'll drive her mad.'

He gave a grunt of laughter and indicated his bandaged right hand and arm. 'Look at me. How does she imagine that I could—?'

'Like a hedgehog, very carefully.'

He laughed again and winced at the effort. When they were safely in the flat he collapsed on to the sofa.

'Why didn't you say you were in pain?' she demanded.

'Damn fool pride, I suppose. I've been practising exercises with my arm. I may have overdone it a bit.'

'More than a bit. Have you taken your pain-killers?'

'No, I thought it was time I tried to manage without them.'

'Damn fool pride is right. Let the doctors decide that.'

She brought him a glass of mineral water and two of his pills, which he swallowed gratefully.

'I think you should go to bed,' she said. 'Come on, I'll help you.'

He put an arm around her shoulders and together they went into the bedroom. With impersonal hands she undressed him down to his shorts, helped to ease him on to the pillows, and drew the duvet up over him.

'Sorry,' he said with a sigh.

'Don't be silly,' she said, sitting on the bed beside him. 'It's partly my fault. I shouldn't have let you go to that party.'

'Think you could have stopped me?'

'I could have knocked you out.'

'Nah! Never repeat yourself.'

She smiled at his game attempt at humour. 'Shall I go away and let you sleep?'

'No, stay and talk to me,' he whispered.

'What about?'

'Did you really say it?'

'Say what?' she asked, puzzled.

He was silent and she thought he must have fallen asleep, but then, still with his eyes closed, he said, 'Not again!'

'Luke—?'

He opened his eyes.

'You said, "Oh, God, not again!" Or did I dream that? I was pretty much out of it, but I thought I heard you.'

Now she knew what he meant. In the shock of seeing him lying on the floor, covered in blood, she'd gathered him in her arms and had felt herself wrenched back to that other time. For a terrible moment she hadn't known which of them she held.

Her throat constricted and she couldn't speak. She

dropped her head into her hands and stayed there, her eyes closed, in torment, until she felt his good hand brush her hair.

'Tell me.'

'I can't,' she said hoarsely.

'Minnie, you must tell someone, or you'll go mad. What is it that you've been hiding for so long? Why can't you speak of it?'

'Because I can't,' she said passionately. 'I just can't.'

'Trust me, *carissima*. You can tell me anything. Just trust me as a friend.'

He thought she would refuse again, but then a shudder went through her and she raised her head. Her eyes were full of tears, and he wasn't sure that she could see him. But after a moment she took a deep breath, and began to tell him everything.

CHAPTER NINE

'I LOVED Gianni,' she said softly. 'I loved him with all my heart and soul. We were close in every way a man and woman can be close. We laughed at the same jokes, saw the world through the same eyes, and when we made love, everything was perfect.

'But in the last year things started to go wrong. My career had suddenly taken off and I had to devote a lot more time to it. He'd never minded before but he began to mind about my being away from home so often. And even when I was here I had to do a lot of work. He resented it, and we began to quarrel.

'In the end we seemed to do almost nothing but bicker. We tried to set aside some time for ourselves, we planned a big meal—we were going to cook it together—it was going to make everything right. But at the last minute I was called out to see a client. We had a terrible fight. He said if I went out now we were finished, he never wanted to see me again. I said that suited me fine because I'd had enough of him.

'I ran out, to go to my client. He called after me, then ran down the stairs into the street. I heard him but I didn't even look behind, I was so angry. So I didn't hear what happened, I only heard the crash and people screaming.'

She stopped, shuddering. Silently Luke reached up to curve his arm around her and draw her down against him.

'Go on,' he said sombrely.

'When I heard that terrible noise, I did look back. Gianni was lying on the ground, blood pouring from his head. He'd been hit by a truck. I ran back. He was lying so still and his eyes were closed, but I wouldn't let myself believe he could be dead. I had so much to say to him that I *had* to make him hear. I knelt beside him and lifted him in my arms, telling him I was sorry, I hadn't meant what I said, I loved him. I kept screaming over and over again that I loved him, but he couldn't hear.'

Her words ended in a gasp. Tears were pouring down her face, and he tightened his arm, letting his lips rest on her hair, but saying nothing.

'I did love him,' she sobbed. 'I didn't mean any of those things I said, and I was going to say sorry when I came home. But when I tried to tell him, he couldn't hear me. The last thing he heard me say was that I'd had enough of him—that was the last thing—the last thing—'

An anguished wail broke from her as her control collapsed, letting misery break through in a fierce stream that blotted out the world. There were no words now, just a wail that went on and on, as endless as her grief.

'Minnie—' he whispered. 'Minnie—Minnie—'

'It was the last thing he heard,' she screamed. 'I told him I was sorry—I told him again and again but he couldn't hear—he was dead and now he'll never know—'

The wail came again, punctuated by violent sobs that shook her until Luke feared she would break apart. He held on to her, cursing his own helplessness, feeling her grief become his own agony.

'It wasn't your fault,' he said, knowing that the reasonable words were worse than useless. All he could do was hold her against him, letting the warmth of his body communicate comfort, and hoping it would somehow reach her.

He was a man of action, who took firm decisions and saw things through to the end. Now he was all at sea, floundering, trying to achieve something that wasn't in his power, desperate at his own uselessness.

He didn't speak again, just rested his cheek against her hair, waiting for the storm to pass. Gradually her sobs subsided into a soft moan.

'It was my fault,' she said at last.

'What do you mean? How can it be?'

'If I'd gone back when he first called me—it wouldn't have happened. I could have stopped it—he'd be alive now—'

'Minnie, don't think like that,' he begged. 'It's the way to madness.'

'I know. I've gone mad, and come back and gone mad. In my dreams it happens all over again, but this time I turn around and go back, and he's safe, and he stays alive. And then I wake and he's dead, and I go mad again.'

She was clutching his arm, her fingers digging in so tightly that he winced with pain, but he didn't try to pull away. Nothing would have made him move at this moment.

'I keep thinking that if only I could turn time back, and stop it in the right place—' she whispered.

'I know, I know—'

'I try and try, but it goes on without me, and there's nothing I can do.'

'There never is,' he said sadly. 'Finality is the hardest thing to accept. There's nothing to be done, and you can beat yourself senseless trying.'

'Yes,' she said. 'But being senseless would be a relief. It's remembering that's torture.'

'What do the others in the family say? Surely they don't blame you?'

'They don't know. Nobody knows.'

'Dear God!' he whispered, appalled by her isolation.

'Nobody else heard what we said. Several people saw him chase me down the stairs and out into the road, but they didn't know we were quarrelling. They think he was trying catch me up because I'd forgotten something, or he wanted to give me a final kiss. I've never been able to tell Netta the truth, not just for my own sake, I swear it, but because it would add to her pain. She can just about cope with thinking it was an accident—'

'It *was* an accident.'

'No, it wasn't,' she said with bitter self-condemnation. 'It happened because I was angry and cruel and—'

'Stop it!' he said fiercely. 'Stop it, don't talk like that. You're not to blame. It was just one of those terrible flips of the coin that happen without warning. It destroyed him, but it's come near to destroying you, too.'

'Yes,' she agreed bleakly. 'Sometimes I look at Netta and wonder what she'd think if she knew the truth. She's kind to me and I want to tell her that I don't deserve it.'

'But you do. You deserve kindness and love and everything that's good. How can I convince you?'

She didn't answer for a long time, and then she simply repeated, 'He'll never know,' in a broken whisper. 'I've tried to tell him so often since. Just before the funeral I saw him in his coffin and I told him that I loved him and I was sorry, but it was no use. It wasn't him. He was cold and grey like a waxwork and I couldn't see my Gianni because he'd gone somewhere I couldn't follow.'

A memory came back to him.

'That day when I saw you at his grave—'

'We go there on anniversaries, his birthday, the day he died—I'd rather go alone but Netta likes it to be a family party.'

'Yes, I remember, it almost looked like a party. The boys were telling him jokes.'

'That's how it is. Gianni's still one of the family. They talk as though he were there. They still love him, like they still love me, and I feel such a fraud.'

'And when you all went away, you turned to look back at him, and I saw your face. Everything you've just told me was there, only I didn't understand.'

'I knew you'd seen me, with the truth written all over me, and I hated you for it.'

'Don't hate me,' he begged. 'Minnie don't—don't, please—'

'How can I ever hate you? I've trusted you with something that nobody else in the world knows, and I still don't understand why.'

She spoke like a puzzled child and he knew a sudden surge of protectiveness.

'Because you know in your heart that you *can* trust me,' he said. 'I'm your friend, and I won't let you down. I'm here to take care of you.'

'It's supposed to be me looking after you,' she said, changing her position so that she could prop herself on her elbows and look directly at him.

Her face was still ravaged, and running with tears that she no longer seemed to notice. He stroked his fingers tentatively over her cheeks.

'We'll have to look after each other,' he said fondly, 'in different ways.'

'Can I get you anything before you settle down for the night?' she asked. She gave a little choke and tried to pull herself together.

'No, I'm all right. The pills are working now. But what about you? I don't think you're all right.'

'I'm fine, honestly. Sorry I made such a fuss.'

'You're not making a fuss. Your whole life is going to be ruined if we can't make this go away.'

'It'll never go away,' she said simply. 'It'll always be there, and the only way I can cope is to live with it.'

'But live with it how? By being overwhelmed with

guilt? Minnie, you can't spend your life atoning for something that wasn't your fault.'

'Why not? His life was taken away from him because of me. What right do I have to a life?'

'Or to happiness?' he asked angrily. 'Or to love? His life was *his* life, and it's over. You can't prolong it by sacrificing the rest of yours.'

She shook her head and tried to pull away, but he held on to her.

'Minnie—'

'Let me go, I shouldn't have told you.'

'Yes, you should, because I'm the one person who can let the light of day into this. *Trust me, Minnie!*'

His voice was commanding and imploring at the same time, because something told him they were at a turning point and everything hung on this moment. She had turned to him but now she was turning away, and he knew he mustn't let it happen.

Suddenly she went limp, as though all the fight had gone out of her, and he was able to draw her against him again.

'Stay here,' he said, commanding now. 'You don't need to fetch me anything, so stay with me.'

'All right,' she said in a muffled voice. 'Just for a few minutes.'

He could feel her body relaxing against him, as though she'd just found something she was waiting for, and in another moment she was asleep.

For a while he listened to her steady breathing, scarcely daring to hope that she had finally found a little peace. He wished he could see her face, but it was enough that she lay there, content and unafraid, in his arms.

He could almost have laughed to think how he'd yearned to have her in his bed, her body pressed against his. Now he had his wish, while at the same time being further away from it than ever. Yet he'd been granted something else, infinitely more sweet and precious, and full of hope.

His good arm ached from being trapped in one position, but nothing would have made him move and disturb her. So he stayed as he was, drifting slowly off to sleep, until he awoke in the small hours to find that the arm was numb, and she hadn't moved by so much as an inch.

Minnie's first sight on waking was the window of her bedroom, just as it had always been. But as memory came back she realised that she was in the wrong place. She should be sleeping in the spare room.

Only then did she become aware of Luke's body pressed against hers, his warmth reaching her through the thickness of the duvet that was between them, his good arm beneath her, his bad arm covering her protectively.

Moving carefully, she raised herself and turned, to find him regarding her from sleepy eyes, just as she'd last seen him before she'd fallen asleep. It was as though he hadn't slept at all, but had spent the night watching over her.

'Are you all right?' were his first words.

'Yes, I'm fine,' she said, realising that it was true. 'Goodness, is that the time?'

It was seven in the morning. Reluctantly, she disentangled herself and rose from the bed, wandering out of the room, too preoccupied to think where she was going. She realised that she was still fully dressed, and memories of the night before began to come back to her.

She had brought him home to look after him, but somehow he'd ended up looking after her. He'd done what nobody else could do, had drawn her agonising secret from her into the light of day, had given her a feeling of peace and strength that she hadn't known for four years.

But it was more than that. In his arms she'd slept like a baby, with no dreams, and this morning she felt well and strong. A healing had begun in her, and that it should be Luke, of all people, who'd brought it about, filled her with wonder.

Most wondrous of all was the fact that he'd held her all night without making a single move that couldn't have been made by a brother, or a nurse. She'd been deeply asleep, but instinct told her that she'd been safe and protected in his arms.

He didn't try to make love to me, she thought, smiling. *That's the best thing of all, but nobody else would understand.*

He'd said, 'Your whole life is going to be ruined if we can't make this go away.'

We! Not you, but we—the two of us, acting together as friends and allies.

She went to look out of the window on to the staircase where there were already signs of life. Behind her she could hear Luke moving about until he finally joined her. He was moving his left arm gingerly.

'I'm sorry. Did I keep it trapped all night?' she said fondly.

'Don't worry, I'll regain the use of it one day soon.'

They laughed together, and the warmth she felt was quite different from the sensual excitement of kissing him. It was the warmth of safety, and it made her realise anew how long she'd been without it.

Over breakfast he said, 'I wish you didn't have to go out today.'

It was a casual friendly remark, but it carried a new meaning now. She, too, was reluctant to step outside the magic circle they had created.

'I wish I didn't, too. But I've got a big trial coming up. I'm defending someone in a case that should never have been brought in the first place. It's a try-on. They're hoping to scare him into paying them off, and I'm not going to let them.'

'So you're going into battle?' he said.

'That's right. And I may not be very good company when I'm here, so—'

'Minnie, it's all right,' he said quickly. 'You've promised to defend this man and you should give it all you've got.'

Her smile was full of relief, and it hurt him to see it.

He used her absence to make some urgent calls, several to the bank and one to a man the bank had found for him. His name was Eduardo Viccini. He called on Luke that afternoon, and they spent several hours going through papers and discussing tactics.

He had expected Minnie to be late following her day in court, but she was home for supper, and only just missed the visitor by minutes. Luke breathed a sigh of relief. He wasn't ready for Minnie to meet Eduardo Viccini.

She came in smiling, carrying a heavy bag, which she dumped on to the sofa, and followed it, bouncing up and down gleefully.

'You look like a kid let out of school,' he said with a grin.

'That's how I feel. Free! Free!'

'Your case can't be over already.'

'But it is. The other side backed down. They thought we were going to crack but we didn't, and they withdrew. I told you it was a try on. My client will get his costs, the other side gets a great big debt that they've run up with their lawyers, and it serves them right. And I get a holiday because I set aside time for a trial that isn't going to take place. *Free!*'

She threw her arms up in the air.

'Does that mean you can have a rest?' he asked.

'Well, I've got paperwork and stuff to catch up on, but I can relax a bit, yes. And do you know the best thing of all? Someone told me that they heard my legal opponent say they'd done a clever thing to back down rather than face me, because I was a Rottweiler. Isn't that wonderful?'

'Is it?' Luke asked blankly.

'Well, not normally of course, but in my job it's a great compliment.'

'I can see how it would be,' he said, amused. 'Then let's celebrate your freedom. I'll go out and buy some wine and a couple of ready-cooked pizzas. No cooking tonight, just relaxing—'

'And watching some stupid game show on TV?' she asked eagerly.

'The stupider the better,' he promised.

He returned a few minutes later, bearing food and wine, to find her changed out of her severe clothes into jeans and sweater, and looking like 'urchin' Minnie, the one he preferred.

It was a wonderful evening. Over pizza she entertained him with vivid impressions of her courtroom opponents, which made him laugh.

'You should have been an actress,' he said. 'You have the gift.'

'Of course. That's what a lawyer needs. I can be anything in a courtroom—demure, respectful—'

'Or Avvocato Rottweiler,' he supplied.

She gave a reminiscent smile. 'The first time I was in an Italian court, it sounded so strange to hear the lawyers called *Avvocato*. I'd just returned here from England and it sounded like "avocado". I kept giggling and nearly got thrown out.'

'Things never sound so impressive in English,' he said. 'Take your noble ancestor, Pepino il Breve. You've got to admit that "Pepin the Short" lacks a certain something.'

'My noble ancestor!' she scoffed, then began to chuckle. 'Pepin the Short. I love it.'

Afterwards they sat on the sofa and hunted through the TV channels for the worst game shows they could find. There was plenty of choice and they bickered amiably, engaging in furious argument over the sillier questions.

Neither of them had mentioned their closeness of the night before, but when he laid his hand on her arm it seemed natural for her to lie down lengthways, with her feet over the end of the sofa, and her head resting on his leg.

'You got that last one wrong,' she said, taking a bite out of an apple.

'I did not,' he said hotly. 'There were three choices—'

'And you got the wrong one,' she insisted.

'You don't know what you're talking about. The first contestant said—'

'Oh, shut up and hand me another apple.'

He did so and she tucked into it until, a few minutes later, she began to laugh.

'Pepin the Short,' she said. 'What a name!'

'That's what you get for being English,' he said lazily.

'Half English.'

'How did that work out when you were a child?'

'Not well. I don't think my parents' marriage was very happy. My mother was a rather uptight person, while my father, as far as I remember him, was very—very *Italian*, emotional, with a big warm heart and a way of not letting himself be bothered by details. It drove Mamma mad, and I suppose she was right really, because it meant a lot of burdens fell on her. But I didn't see that. I just saw that he was wonderful, and she disapproved of all the things I thought nicest about him.

'When I was eight he died, and she took me back to England as fast as she could. But I could never be at home there. By that time I had an Italian heart and I hated the way she tried to make me completely English, as though she could wipe out my Italian side just by fighting it hard enough. I wasn't allowed to speak Italian or read Italian books, but I did anyway. I used to get them from the library and smuggle them into the house. I can be terribly stubborn.'

'Really? You?'

'Oh, don't be funny. Anyway, you haven't seen me at my worst.'

'Heaven help me!'

'I'll chuck something at you in a minute.'

'You wouldn't assault an invalid, would you?'

'I might if it was you.'

'Go on with your story while I'm still safe.'

'Luckily my mother married again when I was eighteen, and I was clearly in the way, so I could flee back to Italy without anyone trying to stop me. In fact—'

Suddenly a wry grin twisted her mouth.

'What did you do?' he asked, fascinated.

'I don't want to tell you; it's rather shocking,' she admitted.

'You never did anything shocking.'

'Don't you call blackmail shocking?'

'Blackmail?'

'Well, in a sort of way. Although I think bribery is probably a better word. My stepfather was very well-off and he let it be known that if I'd make myself scarce it would put him in a generous mood. I knew I'd need some help until I found my feet—'

Luke began to laugh. 'How much did you take him for?'

'Let's just say it covered my training.'

'Good for you!'

'Yes, I was quite pleased with myself in an insufferable sort of way.'

'Insufferable, nothing! You were smart. If you ever get tired of law I could use you in my business. Come to think of it, the business could use a good lawyer.'

'Ah, then I have to admit that I gave it all back.'

'Minnie, *please!*' he said in disgust. 'Just when I was admiring you! Now you've spoiled it.'

'I know. I tried not to. It was a fair bargain because we each gained from it, and I'd kept my side and never troubled them since. But when I was earning enough to repay it, I just had to. I was really cross with myself.'

He didn't speak for a while. He was fighting an inner battle, sensing the ghost hovering on the edge of their consciousness, unwilling to spoil the moment by inviting him in, yet knowing that he must do so, if he were to be any use to her.

At last he forced himself to say, 'What did Gianni think?'

CHAPTER TEN

HE WAITED to see if she flinched at Gianni's name, but she merely gave a fond, reminiscent smile.

'Gianni thought I was crazy but he didn't try to stop me. Come to think of it, that was always the way. He was very easygoing. He used to say, "You do it your way, *carissima*."' She gave a brief laugh. 'So I always did.'

'He sounds the ideal husband,' Luke observed, keeping his voice carefully light. 'You said, "Jump" and he jumped. What more could a woman ask?'

'Sure, it makes me sound like a domineering wife, but actually it was all a con trick. He pretended to be meek and helpless but it was just a way of pushing the boring jobs on to me. If there were forms to be filled in, phone calls to be made to officials, it was always, "You do it, *cara*. You're the clever one." And after a while it dawned on me that I'd been tricked into doing all the work.'

'Did you mind?'

'Not really. It made sense since I was a lawyer, and you know what bureaucracy is like in this country.'

'And if you hadn't been a lawyer?'

'He'd have found some other excuse, of course,' she said, smiling. 'He was just like my father. Anything not to fill in a form! But so what, as long as one of us could do it? We were a team, a partnership.'

'And you *were* the clever one, weren't you? Cleverer than him, I mean.'

140

'He used to laugh and say anyone was cleverer than him. Sometimes I'd rebel and say, "Come on, you can do that one yourself," and he'd grin and say, "It was worth a try, *cara*." But I didn't mind because he gave me so much in return, love and happiness. We had a marriage that—I don't know—I can't say.'

'Go on,' he said when she fell silent. 'Tell me how it was.'

She shook her head.

'Mind my own business?' he asked lightly.

'We were married for ten years. How can I tell you how "it" was? Which "it" are we talking about? The first year, when we were discovering each other, or the middle years when we settled into being an old married couple?'

'You mean when you were in your mid-twenties? That sort of old?'

'That's right. I didn't mind being "that sort of old" because I knew I'd come home and found the place I belonged. I wanted to stay there for ever.'

'But you can't. Life moves on.'

'I know,' she said with a sigh. 'At first we fitted together perfectly. I spent years going to law school and then serving an apprenticeship with a firm, not earning very much, and he didn't earn very much either.'

'What sort of job did he do?'

'He drove a truck for a local firm that buys a lot of stuff through Naples and Sicily.'

'So he was away a lot?'

'If it was Naples he could get back the same day, even if it was quite late. For Sicily he'd have to be away overnight, maybe two.'

'But that must have been handy if you were studying?'

'It was. He used to say that all the other drivers worried about leaving their wives, in case they were unfaithful, but he knew his only rival was my books.'

'What about children? Did you ever think of having any?'

Was it his imagination, or did she hesitate a moment?

'We talked about it, but there were always hurdles to clear first. I wanted to give him children. He had such a great heart; he'd have been a wonderful father.'

She didn't say any more and he left it there. Another show was coming up on television and they watched it for a while, making ribald comments about the quality of the contestants. She went into the kitchen to create a late night snack, then checked the curtains to make sure that they were completely closed.

'They weren't looking in, were they?' Luke asked.

'I wouldn't put it past them. Once Netta's set her heart on something, she doesn't give up.'

'Couldn't you just be strong, and tell her that nothing on earth would prevail on you to marry me?' he suggested.

'I've already done that. It didn't work. The way she sees it, our marriage would benefit everyone, so it's my duty to sacrifice myself.'

'Thanks!'

She grinned. 'I just thought I'd warn you of the forces ranged against you.'

'Think I can't manage for myself, huh?'

'Are you kidding? Between you and Netta I'd back her any day.'

'So would I,' he observed gloomily.

'Don't worry; I'll save you from that ghastly fate. I'll be strong for both of us.'

'Who's strong for you?' he asked impulsively. 'Who's ever done that?'

Her shrug seemed to imply that she had no need, but he was beginning to know better.

The game show was followed by a historical film, made about fifty years ago and set in the days of ancient chivalry. It concerned a knight escorting a lady to her wedding with a great lord. They fell in love but maintained perfect virtue, symbolised by the knight laying his sword on the ground between them as they slept side by side.

People said 'Gadzooks!' and 'Avaunt!' The lady swooned regularly. The colour was lurid and the film was truly terrible. They enjoyed it immensely.

'If you tried that sword trick in real life,' Luke observed, 'you'd be cut to pieces.'

'And they're all so clean,' Minnie objected. 'Days travelling through the countryside, and not a speck. Do you want anything else to eat?'

'No, thanks,' he said, yawning. 'I'm off to bed.'

'Me, too.'

In the doorway he paused and said lightly, 'I don't have a sword, but I do have a bad arm.'

'You don't have to reassure me,' she said quietly.

'I'll see you, then.'

When she appeared in his room a few minutes later he was in bed. He extended his good left arm and she tucked herself into the crook. He turned out the light, and for a while she was so still that he thought she'd fallen asleep. But then she said, 'Thank you, Luke.'

'Does it help?' he asked quietly.

'You'll never know how much.'

She fell asleep on the words. He waited, listening to her soft breathing in the darkness. At last, easy in his mind about her, he settled down.

Only once in the night did she stir and begin muttering

words that he could not discern. He stroked her hair with his bandaged hand, murmuring, 'It's all right. I'm here.'

She became content, and didn't move again.

Sometimes over the next few nights, lying in the darkness of that quiet room, Minnie had the feeling of being in a small boat that was drifting out into uncharted sea. Their destination was a mystery, but she knew there was nothing to fear.

She had no idea what deep instinct had made Luke so attuned to her needs, and so willing to subordinate everything else to her. This man whom she'd once thought harsh and insensitive, seemed to have the power to look into her heart, and be gentle with what he found there.

She lost track of time. By day they talked, or rather she talked while he listened, offering the odd word or question to bring forth more memories that always looked strangely different once she had voiced them. He had spoken of letting in the light of day, and it was true. At night there was the comfort of untroubled sleep.

It couldn't last. The passion that had briefly flared was still there, subdued but waiting. But, for now, this was the sweetest experience of her life.

She lost track of time. She only knew that one night his cellphone, which he kept beside the bed, shrilled until they woke. He fumbled for it, tried to press the right button with his left hand, and dropped it.

'Stay,' she said, motioning him back while she picked up the phone, pressed the button, and handed it to him.

He grunted his thanks. *'Pronto!'*

It was Toni, and Luke could hear at once that something was badly wrong. Minnie, watching, heard him say 'Mamma!' twice, and grow pale.

'I'll be there as fast as I can,' he said, and hung up.

'What's happened?'

'It's my mother,' he said, speaking with difficulty. 'She collapsed suddenly and had to be rushed to hospital. They think it's a heart attack and she might—I've got to get there, fast.'

'I'll call the airport,' Minnie said at once.

But the flight from Rome to Naples had just left, and there wasn't another until the following morning.

'It'll be midday before I land,' he groaned. 'That might be too late. I'll have to drive.'

'Not with that bandaged hand,' Minnie said. 'You'll never control a car.'

'Don't you understand? I have to get there!' he raged.

'Then I'll take you. The roads will be clear at this hour, and we'll be there in less than three hours.'

Without giving him a chance to answer, she went to her room and dressed quickly. When she came out he'd managed to scramble into some clothes and was standing by the door, his whole being expressive of tense urgency.

Her car was locked in a row of garages further down the street. As quickly as she could, she eased it out, and soon they were on their way out of Rome, on to the *autostrada* that led to Naples. Then she put her foot down, driving as fast as she dared.

Only once during the journey to Naples did he speak. 'Thank you. I don't know how I'd have managed but for you.'

'Anyone in that building would have done this for you,' she said. 'They all count you as their friend. But I wanted to be the one to do it.'

'Thank you,' he said again, and fell into brooding silence.

On the outskirts of Naples they came to a place where there had been an accident. Nobody had been hurt, but a truck lay on its side, blocking the road, save for one lane, and the traffic had slowed to a standstill.

Luke groaned and seized his cellphone. But his father's phone was switched off.

'Hospitals won't have them on,' Minnie said sympathetically. 'But we'll be there soon. The front of this queue is moving.'

He slumped down in his seat. 'It might be too late. *Why wasn't I there?*'

'Has she been ill before?'

'Not as far as I know.'

'Then how could you have been on the alert? You couldn't have known this was going to happen.'

'That's easy to say, but she might be dead right this minute, and I wouldn't know. I should have called her more often. She might have told me that she was feeling bad—'

'But maybe she wasn't. Luke, don't start creating "what ifs?" to torment yourself.'

'But you can't stop yourself creating them,' he said sombrely. 'You know that better than anyone. Suddenly I find myself saying all the things you said about Gianni.'

'But you didn't quarrel with her,' she said softly. 'She knows you love her.'

'I should have called her yesterday, but I didn't. If I had, I'd have said—' he sighed heavily '—probably nothing very much, but she'd have known I cared because I took the time to make the call.'

She longed to comfort him, as he had comforted her. The traffic was still for the moment, and, in her desperation to pierce his haze of misery, she took hold of him and gave him a little shake, forcing him to look at her.

'Luke, listen to me. How many years has she been your mother? More than thirty? Do you think she doesn't know by now how you feel about her? Do you think one incident counts against all those years?'

'Why not?' he asked her simply. 'Isn't that what you think about Gianni? All those years of loving him, and you can't forgive yourself for one incident.'

'But you've been telling me how wrong I was.'

'I know. And you *are* wrong, just as I'm wrong now. And we both know it, but it doesn't help, does it?'

'No,' she said, putting her arms right round him. 'It doesn't help, however hard we try to reason, because in the end reason has nothing to do with it. It's what you feel.'

'If she dies—'

'It's too soon to say that.'

'If she dies before I can speak to her—then I shall really understand what you've been going through, instead of just talking about it. Oh, Minnie, what an idiot you must have thought me! All talk, knowing nothing.'

'It wasn't like that. You gave me so much—more than you'll ever know. But it wasn't the words, it was that you were there, all the time. That was what I needed most. Now *I'm* here. Hold on to me.'

His grip was painful, but she was glad of it. It was all she could do for him, to offer back a little of what he had given, and pray that in the end he wouldn't need any of it.

'The line's moving again,' she said. 'We'll be there soon.'

She kissed him again and again. 'Just a little longer. Hold on.'

He nodded. She could see tears in his eyes, and it was with reluctance that he released her.

A policeman was waving them on. She started up and

began moving at a crawl until at last they were past the accident, the road widened and she was free to drive on.

'You'll have to guide me from here,' she said.

He gave her the name of the hospital and directed her until the huge building came into view.

'I'll drop you at the main door, then go and park the car,' she said. 'I'll find you afterwards.'

His answer was a tense smile, and she knew he was fearing to hear the worst. As she drew up outside the main door, she reached over and gave his left hand a squeeze.

'Good luck,' she said.

His answer was a return squeeze, then he got out quickly and hurried into the building.

At that time of night the parking lot was almost empty. She parked without trouble and followed him into the hospital, where the man on the night desk directed her to the third floor. Upstairs she found herself in a corridor of private rooms. Turning a corner, she stopped at the sight that met her eyes.

A crowd of young men were standing, sitting or lounging close to one door. Two were young and handsome, with a definite facial resemblance, one was older, with the same resemblance, but less marked. It was enough to tell her that these were the Rinuccis.

They all seemed to notice her at the same time, and moved quickly towards her in a way that could have been alarming if they hadn't been so clearly friendly.

'Signora Pepino—Luke told us—we have been expecting you—you brought our brother here—*grazie, grazie*—'

Hand after hand clasped hers with vigour. It was overwhelming, yet powerfully attractive.

'What's the news of your mother?' she asked quickly.

'It's good,' said one of the men. 'I am Primo Rinucci.'

'Good—how?' she asked. 'I understood it was a heart attack.'

One of the handsome boys spoke up. 'Mamma was breathless and then she fainted, so we got her here, fast. The doctor says it was only a dizzy spell, but she must take better care of herself in case the next time is more serious. So we're going to make sure that she does take care.'

'But still we thank you for what you have done.' This was the other good-looking boy.

There was a chorus of agreement and they all swarmed around her again, this time embracing and kissing her. Now it felt like coming home, she thought. Being embraced by Rinuccis was like being embraced by Pepinos—pleasant and comforting.

The door opened and a man in late middle age appeared. Over his shoulder Minnie could see Luke sitting by the bed, his mother's hands clasped in his. Then he was shut off from her sight. The young men called him Pappa, and rushed to introduce her. This was Toni Rinucci, whose face bore the marks of a night of strain and fear, although it was gradually clearing.

He, too, thanked her, almost fiercely, and answered her question about his wife's health with a passionate, 'The doctors say she will be well, thank God! And you must forgive me for dragging you on this long journey, but I am her husband—I panic because I love her.'

'How could you not panic?' she agreed, nodding.

'All of our sons will be here soon,' he told her. 'Justin is coming from England, Franco is in America and will be here later today. My wife will feel better for having her whole family around her. She will want to meet you, too, but in the meantime you'll be wanting to get some rest. Carlo and Ruggiero will take you to our home.'

'Can we see Mamma first?' Carlo said.

'No, she can't have too many people in there at once, and this is Luke's time. Be off now, and look after our guest.'

'Let Carlo take your car,' Ruggiero said as they left the hospital, 'and I'll drive you in mine. It's not far. You'll see the house before we've gone a mile.'

She did see it, high on the hill, gleaming with lights that seemed to reach down to them as they climbed. As they drew into the wide courtyard a middle-aged woman came out to wait for them.

'That's Greta, our housekeeper,' Ruggiero said. 'Pappa will have called ahead and she will have prepared a room for you.'

Inside the house they thanked her again for bringing Luke, and she followed Greta up the stairs to her room. She accepted the refreshments the housekeeper offered, but she was longing to be alone to sort out her thoughts. It had all happened so suddenly that she was almost dizzy.

She had a shower in the little bathroom. It washed off the worst of the night, but she still felt the need to lie down for a nap.

When she awoke the sun was high in the sky, and her window showed her a car gliding up the hill. When it drew to a halt below she saw Luke and his father get out. They were smiling in a way that confirmed the good news. For a moment her instinct told her to rush down into his arms, but then she saw the others hurry out to them, heard the cheering, saw them all clap each other on the back.

She wasn't needed there, she realised. Luke was back

with his family, where he belonged. His mother wasn't seriously ill after all, and the moments when they had clung to each other, full of intense, despairing emotion, seemed to come from another world.

She sat down on the bed, feeling a bleak sense of anti-climax.

Since her job sometimes called for her to travel at a moment's notice Minnie kept a bag always ready, containing clean clothes and toiletries. She'd snatched it up before leaving and was glad now that she could dress smartly.

Greta came with coffee and a message to say that lunch was being served below. Luke was waiting for her as she descended the stairs. He looked unshaven but happy, and he enfolded her in an exuberant hug.

'She's all right,' he whispered in her ear. 'She'll be home later today, and she's longing to meet you.'

'She must have got a shock when she saw your bandages.'

'Yes, but I played it down, and she could see I'm all right. She's mad at me for not telling her before, but I'll be forgiven. She'll probably try to pump you for more details—'

'I'll be the soul of discretion,' she promised.

Now she must be introduced to the others, including Primo, whom she had briefly seen in the corridor that morning. She remembered Luke saying, 'Primo had an Italian mother, so he calls me *Inglese*, as an insult.'

And there, with Primo, was Olympia, the black-haired woman of the photograph in Luke's wallet. Meeting her now, Minnie saw that she only had eyes for Primo, and she embraced her willingly.

Carlo was missing and Luke explained that he'd gone to the airport to meet Justin, his wife and son.

'I told you about him,' he reminded her.

'The child who was taken away from her at birth,' Minnie remembered. 'And she thought he was dead.'

'Yes. They were married here a few weeks ago, and now they're barely back from their honeymoon.'

'The house is going to get very crowded. I should be going soon.'

'No way, not until Mamma has met you. She—'

The shrill of his phone interrupted him. He answered impatiently and she heard him say, 'Eduardo? Sorry I had to leave unexpectedly. I can't talk now—I'll call you back.'

He hung up quickly. Minnie was about to ask who Eduardo was when a noise outside caused everyone to rush to the windows to see Justin and his family arrive.

They had to be reassured that Hope was well and would be home later that day, and Minnie stood back while Luke was once more sucked into his family.

It was a fascinating sight, she thought, like watching the missing piece that completed a jigsaw puzzle. Always before she had seen him as an outsider. Now she saw the niche where he fitted. Even so, she could see deep into him now, and tell that the fit wasn't perfect. In part he was still an outsider, from choice.

When she could escape she returned to her room and called Netta, who had been agog with curiosity at finding the two of them missing. She was all sympathy when she heard of Luke's trouble, but added anxiously, 'You will bring him back, won't you, *cara*? You won't let him stay there?'

'Of course not,' she said mechanically, and hung up quickly.

She felt winded. She should have seen this coming. And she hadn't.

It hadn't occurred to Minnie that Luke wouldn't return with her to Rome, but now she saw the danger. For him Rome might be no more than a passing mood, to be put behind him once a convenient opportunity presented itself.

The closeness that had seemed to unite them could turn out to be no more than a chimera now that he was back with his family. They would still correspond about legal matters, but essentially it was over.

CHAPTER ELEVEN

HOPE RINUCCI came home that afternoon. Toni went to collect her, insisting that nobody should come with him, as he wanted to be alone with his wife. When he handed her out of the car she looked well, smiling with pleasure at her family's attention. It was obvious now that it really had been a false alarm.

Watching from the sidelines, Minnie saw an elegant, beautiful woman in her fifties, a woman who would attract admiring attention wherever she went, no matter what her age. She couldn't help smiling as Hope's sons converged on her. It was like watching vassals do homage. She almost expected them to kiss her hand.

One by one she hugged everyone—Justin, her eldest son, Evie, his new wife, and Mark, his son by his first marriage. Then Primo and Olympia.

'We can really get down to planning your marriage,' she told them.

When she'd kissed her twins, Carlo and Ruggiero, she looked around hopefully.

'Franco?'

'Later today, Mamma,' Carlo said. 'It's a long way from Los Angeles.'

At last Hope's eyes sought out the young woman who held back, watching and silent.

'And you are Minnie?' she said.

'Yes, I'm Minnie.'

She came forward to be enveloped in a scented embrace. Hope gave her a genuinely warm hug, then drew back and looked at her.

'Luke has told me how you brought him here,' she said. 'And I thank you with all my heart.'

Minnie, normally so assured, found herself suddenly awkward.

'It was nothing—just a short drive.'

A sudden tension seemed to come over Hope. It was almost indefinable, an extra edge of alertness, a slight turn of her head so that her ear was closer to Minnie, the better to catch a familiar tone.

'Three hours is not a short drive,' she replied, 'especially when you've been torn from sleep. I don't think it was "nothing". Also, Luke has told me how you've been looking after him since the explosion. We must speak more of this later.'

'I'm glad you turned out to be all right, anyway,' Minnie said.

Hope smiled and said something gracious, then gave her attention to Luke, who had been standing by.

Hope refused their suggestion that she should go to bed, insisting that she felt well and wanted only to be among them. Half an hour later a car drew up outside and the missing son appeared. Franco had been in Los Angeles for the last few weeks and had just stepped off the plane after a thirteen hour flight. He and Hope ran straight into each other's arms.

'I always thought he was her favourite,' said Olympia, who was close to Minnie. 'Of course, she'd deny that she has any favourites, but with Franco there's just a little something extra—I think.' Seeing Minnie looking at her, she added, 'With Hope it's never wise to be sure.'

'I can see that she's a very unusual woman,' Minnie agreed.

'She sees everything, she hears everything, she knows everything,' Olympia said. 'And she plots in secret.'

'Plots?'

'She thinks it's time she had more daughters-in-law, and she's not the type to just sit back and cross her fingers. Justin and Evie actually broke up, but she went to England and got them on track again.'

'And you and Primo?'

Olympia chuckled. 'I must admit that it was Luke who played Cupid that time. You wouldn't think it to look at him, would you?'

'He doesn't look like Cupid, no,' Minnie said, regarding Luke with her head on one side, and considering the matter seriously. 'But then, Cupid comes in many shapes. Sometimes he can look like a good friend, until you're ready for more.'

'There's got to be a whole fascinating history behind that remark,' Olympia said.

'There is,' Minnie assured her.

There were more introductions, but Franco was clearly too full of jet lag to take in many details, and he wanted to talk to his mother.

Minnie found an unexpected ally in young Mark, Justin's thirteen year old son, who turned out to come from the same part of London where she'd once lived with her mother. They had a good time saying, 'Do you know that place where—?' until Evie, his step-mother, came to join in.

As soon as dinner was over Minnie said quietly to Luke, 'I'll say goodnight now.'

'So soon?'

'I don't mean to be impolite, but I'm really in the way here. Your mother wants to be with her family, and I should catch up with my emails. I brought my laptop.'

'Do you take work everywhere you go?' he asked, appalled.

'It's always useful.'

She said goodnight to Hope, excusing herself on the grounds of catching up on her lost sleep of the night before.

In her room she connected the laptop and tried to concentrate on work, but it was strangely hard. From below she could heard the hum of a happy family, and it increased the sense of isolation that had swept over her.

I don't belong here, she thought. *I should get back to Naples and 'my' family, who need me.*

Then she wondered at herself for feeling this way. Since Gianni's death she'd taught herself to be self-sufficient, as content alone as in a crowd, and it was natural that she should be an outsider here. But she felt as though she'd been separated from Luke at the very moment that her heart wanted to draw nearer to him.

Jealousy, she thought, mocking herself. Jealousy at this late date.

And fear lest she lose him, a feeling she'd known so little that it had taken her time to recognise it.

She worked for a couple of hours, subconsciously listening to the house grow quiet about her. Then she shut down the computer, showered and got ready for bed. When the light was out she went to the window and stood looking out over the garden, where coloured lights hung between the trees.

A few yards along from her she could see a staircase leading down to the garden, and suddenly she needed to be down there. There was nobody in the corridor when she looked out, and she hurried along to where a door led out on to a balcony, from where the stairs descended.

In a moment she'd run down on to the lawn, hurrying to get between the trees.

Here there was fresh sea air to be breathed in, and a sense of release. She stood looking down at the bay, taking deep breaths, feeling herself relax after the nervous strains of the last two days. Passionately she longed for Luke to be here with her, but strangely she also longed to get away from here, back to Rome, back to the life she knew and where she belonged, back to the time before she'd met Luke.

She wanted him, yet he threatened something in her, and part of her wanted to flee, all the more because she sensed that he was as wary of her as she was of him.

'Are you there?'

She whirled around to see him coming towards her between the trees, and her own flash of happiness was like a warning. *Get away from him now.*

'Yes, I'm here,' she called back softly.

He reached out and drew her into the shadows with him.

'I was afraid I wouldn't see you again tonight. Did you come out to find me?'

'No, I just—well, maybe I did—'

Hadn't that been in her mind all the time? she wondered.

'I wanted to talk to you all evening,' he murmured, 'but I couldn't get close to you. This place is too crowded. I wish I could come back to Rome with you, but I can't leave just yet.'

She made a wry grimace. 'The flat is going to feel awfully empty without you.'

'Yes, you won't have anyone to tell you the answers in the game shows,' he agreed.

'Or help me with the crossword puzzles.'

'You've got to admit, I have my uses,' he said with a wry attempt at humour.

'Oh, yes—Luke—Luke—'

Minnie reached up to take his face between her hands, looking at him intently, torn by two powerful emotions, full of confusion.

'What is it?' he asked. 'Which of us are you looking at?'

'Luke—don't—'

'Who is it, Minnie? Him or me?'

This time it was she who drew him close. 'Not now,' she whispered.

He wanted to protest that it mattered, but the sweet scent of her was in his nostrils. He'd been strong for her sake, but now it was she who wanted him to be weak and that was harder to fight.

When her lips brushed against his he knew that resisting her wasn't going to be hard, but impossible. The passion he'd thought under control welled up now, so that she was flame in his arms, burning and igniting him, driving him to kiss her with a kind of ruthlessness.

And at once he felt her response to that ruthlessness. She was no green girl but a woman who'd experienced passionate love, but had then lived celibate while desire built in her, waiting to be triggered by the right man. It was all there in the heated movements of her mouth, the sensuality that made her press closer to him, the hot breath that mingled with his.

She offered no resistance when his lips trailed down her neck to the base of her throat, then further to the swell of her breasts. He could feel the pounding of her heart, hear the soft groan that broke from her and everything in him urged him on to what could be a blissful conclusion.

Or disaster.

'Minnie—' He seemed to hear himself say her name as if from a distance. 'Minnie—wait—'

Using all the strength he could find, he drew away and held her at arm's length.

'Wait—' he said again. 'Not like this.'

'What?' she whispered.

'Look at me,' he said urgently. 'Look at me.'

Her face was upturned to him but he saw with alarm that her eyes were unfocused.

'Where are you, Minnie? You're not here with me. *Where are you?' And who's there with you?* he wanted to add.

'Why do you worry about things now?' she whispered.

'Because I want you too much to risk what we could have,' he said hoarsely. 'Or maybe I'm fooling myself and we could never have it—'

'No, you're not fooling yourself but... So much has happened. Luke—if you want me—'

'I do. I want you as much as any man has ever wanted any woman, *but not like this.*'

'What do you mean?'

'Where is Gianni? Can you tell me that?'

There was a stunned look in her eyes, as though she were pulling herself together with an effort.

'He's here, isn't he?' Luke raged. 'He's here because he's always here, but that's not good enough. I want you to come to me, *me*, not some fantasy figure that's half me and half the man you really love.'

He gave a little shake. 'Get rid him,' he growled. 'Or tell me how to get rid of him.'

'I don't know how.' It was a cry of pain.

'You must, if there's ever to be anything for us. I want

to make love to you. God knows how much I want that, but only when I come first with you. Until then—'

A tremor shook him, made up of thwarted desire and rage.

'Until then there's nothing between us,' he managed to say before thrusting her from him and walking away.

It felt brutal, but he had to do it while he still had the strength.

He got as far away from her as possible, but then turned back. He wanted to tire himself, even though he knew it was no cure for what was raging through him. There was only one cure for that, and he began to think he would never find it.

Looking up, he saw a light in Minnie's window. He longed to go up to her room, beg her to forget what had passed tonight, say he would accept anything if only he could find a home in her bed, in her heart.

But this was the most dangerous temptation of all. He ran from it, turning into a path that led away from the house, into the trees, then out again to where he knew there was a garden seat, overlooking the bay. There he could be safely alone.

But someone was there before him.

'Come and sit with me, my son,' Hope invited, patting the space beside her.

He did so, seating himself with a sigh, and running a hand through his hair. Hope watched him, silent but understanding.

'So now I've met your ''chambermaid''?' she said at last, with a twinkle.

'Chambermaid?'

'The one who answered the phone that morning. There now, don't I have a marvellous memory for an old woman?'

'You'll never be old, and I've sometimes wished that your memory was a little less marvellous.'

'I know that. It's quite disconcerting how well I remember certain things. You said she was the chambermaid.'

'Mamma, I didn't actually say that. You suggested it and I—'

'Saw a useful way out,' Hope teased. 'Admit it.'

She was laughing, and after a moment he joined in. 'All right, I'm a coward. No question about it.'

'You may also recall,' Hope said, 'that I heard in her voice that she had a passionate nature. Now I've heard that voice again, and I know I was right.'

'Yes,' he murmured, still trying to calm himself. 'Yes. But Mamma, it's not like that.'

'Perhaps it's time you told me what it *is* like.' Hope came to the point of real importance. 'Am I going to have another daughter-in-law, or not?'

'I don't know,' he admitted. 'It's complicated.'

'Then why not tell me about it?'

'What is this? The Inquisition?'

'Just a mother's curiosity.'

'Is there a difference?'

'Not much,' Hope admitted, patting his hand. 'So, give in and tell me everything without making me work harder.'

'Yes, that was always the easiest way,' he recalled. 'All right, she was in my hotel room, but I wasn't there with her.'

'Then where were you? Tell me.'

'Yes, tell us,' said a voice from the shadows, and they both looked up to see Olympia standing there with a glass of champagne in her hand. She strolled forward and settled herself on a fallen tree trunk that lay nearby, and looked at their faces.

'I'm all ears to hear where you were,' she said.

'The trouble with acquiring a sister,' Luke said with careful restraint, 'is that it's just one more female to put her nose into a man's private affairs.'

'Good, then I'm doing the right thing,' Olympia said gleefully. 'Come on, tell. Where were you?'

Luke took a deep breath. There was no putting this off any longer.

'I was in a police cell,' he said through gritted teeth.

If this disconcerted his mother she gave no sign of it, merely nodding her head as if to say that sooner or later every young man saw the inside of a police cell. Which was probably what she did actually believe. Olympia contented herself with a little choke of laughter.

'What were you doing there?' she asked mildly.

'I got involved in a brawl and was arrested. Charlie was brawling too—he's Minnie's brother-in-law.'

'And his name's Charlie?' Olympia asked.

'It short for Charlemagne, because the family name is Pepino, which was the name of Charlemagne's father—'

'And they're descended from him?' Hope said.

Luke grinned. 'You'd never get them to admit that they weren't. And one of the neighbours has a cat called Tiberius—'

'After the Emperor Tiberius?' Hope asked, her lips twitching.

'Of course. It's that sort of place.'

He began to laugh at the memory, unaware that his mother was looking at him with fascination.

'So you and Charlemagne were brawling,' she reminded him.

'And Minnie came to bail him out, and that's how we met. She ended up defending me in court as well.'

The two women burst into laughter.

'How I wish I'd been there to see,' Hope said at last. 'My sensible, businesslike son, in a drunken brawl!'

'I didn't say drunken—'

'Nonsense, of course it was!' Olympia said firmly. 'Oh, dear—'

They went off into more gales of laughter while Luke gritted his teeth. But after a moment he relaxed and grinned.

'I remember the day you left here,' Hope said, 'full of plans to confront her in a businesslike fashion, not standing for any nonsense—'

'And I did confront her, in a police cell, with my clothes torn. I didn't have my ID card so she had to go to the hotel to collect it, and my phone. That's how she came to answer it.'

'You've been keeping a lot to yourself. You told me that you'd moved into the Residenza, but you left out the best things.'

'Well, I wasn't going to boast about my criminal record to my mother,' he said defensively, but he was grinning again.

'But the two of you have made friends now, since she was the one you went to when Toni called.'

He hesitated. 'I didn't have to go to her, Mamma. She was right there with me—'

'In your bed?'

'Her bed. I've been staying with her so that she could nurse me, but it wasn't—as you think.'

'I think nothing, my son, since nothing in your relationship with this young woman seems to follow a normal course. Where do you stand with each other?'

'I only wish I knew. I feel closer to her than any other woman I've ever known, and I know that she needs me. But I'm not the man she loves.'

Hope's eyebrows rose. 'Loving another man, she shares your bed?'

'Not in the sense you mean. For the last week she's cuddled up to me at night as she might have cuddled up to an old dog. The man she loves is her late husband, Gianni Pepino. He's been dead for four years but it might be yesterday, she's still so tied to his memory. No, he's more than a memory, he's a ghost that she can't escape. He's in her thoughts, he's there with us all the time. At night I've held her in my arms while she spoke of him.'

'And that's really all?' Hope asked, incredulous and slightly scandalised at the same time.

'Yes, it makes me sound like a wimp, doesn't it? All right, I *am* a wimp, but it's what she needs. She must talk of him or go mad, and she can't tell the others, so it has to be me.'

'And that is all the use she has for you, my son?'

Luke gave a wry laugh. 'That is all the use she has for me. Tonight, I did briefly hope—but it wasn't me. Not really.'

'But why do you put up with it? There are many other women in the world.'

He said nothing for a moment, but at last he spoke as though with the words he had finally discovered the truth.

'No, Mamma, there aren't. There isn't another woman whose smile can wring my heart as hers can, or make me want to throw aside everything else if only I can make her happy.'

Hope regarded him quizzically. 'This is *you* talking— my son, whose life has been lived balancing the accounts,

calculating what everyone and everything was worth to
him, and taking the long view?'

He winced. 'I'm not as bad as that, am I?'

'You were. But not now, I think.' Then, as though
there were some connection, which perhaps there was,
she added, 'I passed on your message of thanks to
Olympia, by the way.'

'And I'm beginning to understand it now,' Olympia
said. 'At one time you'd never have said the things
you're saying now.'

He nodded. 'At one time, if a woman didn't go my
way, I went off in another direction,' he mused. 'You
were the first one I stuck around for, although I knew I
might be knocked back—and I was. So, when Minnie
knocks me back, I'll have some experience to help me
cope.'

Olympia's answer to this was to lean forward and kiss
him lightly on the mouth.

'I don't think she'll knock you back,' she said. 'Although you may have to come to your big sister for some
advice.'

'Now go on with the story,' Hope commanded. 'Tell
us some more about this man she married.'

'She feels guilty about his death because they were
quarrelling, he chased after her and was run over in the
road. He died in her arms. As a man—' Luke shrugged.
'He seems to have been a good-natured fellow, kind and
affectionate. He was a truck driver, so I doubt if he'd
ever have set the world alight, but he made her feel
loved.'

'Oh-ho!' Hope exclaimed, regarding him with slightly
scornful irony. 'So a truck driver has thrown you into the
shade! You, of course, know all about setting the world

alight, but have you ever made a woman feel so deeply loved that she never recovered from your loss?'

'Never,' he growled. 'There's no need to labour the point, Mamma.'

'No, because you've seen it for yourself, haven't you? You spoke lightly of throwing everything else aside for her sake, but were they only words, or could you live up to them if you had to? You might make her love you in a way, but suppose you can't also drive his ghost away? Can you live with him there, too, for her sake?'

'That's the thought that torments me. Does she love me, or does she merely cling to me from need?'

'And, if it's the second, can you love her anyway? Love isn't like a book-keeping ledger, my son. You don't always get equal repayment in return for what you give. Do you love her enough to settle for less, as long as she is happy?'

'I wish I knew myself better. Tonight we were together out here, and there was a moment when I thought I could make love to her. But I didn't. Something stopped me, something in here—' He laid a hand over his heart.

'What was it that stopped you, my son?'

'He was there and I couldn't get rid of him, and if I can't, how can she? I told her I'd never make love to her until I came first, but—'.

'But suppose you never do?' Olympia asked gently. 'What then?'

He was silent for a long moment, before saying wretchedly, 'I don't know. Heaven help me, *I don't know*!'

Minnie was packed and ready to go next morning.

'Of course you must attend to your work,' Hope told

her kindly, 'but you must return to us soon. Luke, I rely on you to arrange it.'

The others came to bid her goodbye, including Franco, who said, 'You must forgive me for not remembering your name. I was jet lagged out of my mind last night.'

'This is Signora Minerva Pepino,' Luke said.

Only the most astute observer would have noticed the sudden *frisson* that went through Franco. Minnie was too occupied with her troubled thoughts to sense anything.

Luke walked her to the car. 'I'll be in Rome in a day or two,' he said.

'Your mother may want you to stay longer.'

'I can't risk it,' he said lightly. 'Who knows what legal mischief you'll get up to in my absence? I'll be there soon. Count on it.'

'Let's hope they've finished renovating your flat,' she said lightly.

'Are you that anxious to throw me out?'

'Goodbye,' she said, extending her hand and giving him a smile. It contained no warmth, only finality.

'Goodbye,' he said, taking her hand, not knowing what else to say or do.

He watched as she drove away, then walked slowly back to the house.

Franco was on the steps, staring at the road down which Minnie had driven away. He looked puzzled.

'What is it?' Luke asked.

'Nothing, I—did you say her name was Pepino?'

'Yes.'

'Minerva Pepino?'

'That's right. Have you heard of her?'

'I might have. And her husband's name was—?'

'Gianni.'

Franco drew in a sharp breath.

'Whatever's the matter?' Luke asked. 'Did you know Gianni?'

'Not well, but yes, I met him a few times.'

'In Rome?'

'No, here in Naples. He used to come here often.'

'That's right, he collected things in his truck.'

'So he may have done, but he also came to see a woman.'

Luke's head jerked up. 'That's impossible. He was happily married until he died four years ago.'

Franco shrugged. 'Maybe he was, but I'm telling you that he had a woman here, and a son.'

CHAPTER TWELVE

'AND I tell you, you've got it wrong. You're confusing him with someone else.'

'The man I knew was called Gianni Pepino, he had a wife called Minerva and she was a lawyer in Rome.'

Luke poured himself a glass of brandy, and drained it in one gulp. Somewhere inside him an earthquake was taking place.

'I don't believe it,' he murmured. 'She adored him. She still does.'

'Well, he certainly managed to pull the wool over her eyes,' Franco said. 'The girl is called Elsa Alessio, and the child is called Sandro. He got her pregnant when he was down here one summer, fooling around. He was only eighteen, and there was never any talk of marriage. She was older, a divorcee, and she had some money of her own.

'From the way he talked, they weren't in love or anything. They just had a fling and stayed friends. He used to come here to see her and the boy, then go back to Rome. After he got married he just kept on visiting her, chiefly to see his son and give her money—'

'I thought you said she didn't need money.'

'She didn't need to marry him, but a decent man supports his child, and maybe a little extra as a present for her.'

'*Bastardo!*' Luke said softly.

'Why? Gianni loved his wife, and what happened before they married didn't concern her.'

'But he never told her.'

'Of course he didn't. Why hurt her for nothing?'

It was a point of view, Luke realised, with which a lot of men would sympathise. But he was conscious of a burning anger for Minnie's sake.

'How often did he visit her?' he demanded.

Franco shrugged. 'How do I know? But I had a friend who knew him better, and he said Gianni used to boast of those visits.'

'Boast? How?'

Franco shrugged. 'How do you think?'

'Perhaps you should tell us, my son,' Hope said quietly from the shadows.

Franco jumped. 'Mamma. I didn't know you were there.'

'Evidently, or you wouldn't be indulging in foolish, loose talk. Minnie was a guest under our roof. How dare you spread such stories?'

'I didn't invent it, Mamma. It's true.'

'How much is true? About the child? Perhaps.'

'And he boasted that he could have Elsa whenever he wanted,' Franco said.

'And do you know that he was telling the truth? Does one believe every word that a boastful young man says? I don't think so. Listen, my son, you are not to say another word of this matter. Rumours can hurt people, even when they are unfounded, and I would not have Minnie hurt for all the world. Please promise me that you'll forget this and never repeat it.'

'All right, Mamma. I promise.'

'And you'd better keep that promise,' Luke said, 'or I'll throttle you.'

'I've forgotten everything I ever heard, I swear it.'

Looking sheepish, Franco kissed his mother's cheek and departed, careful to avoid Luke's eye.

Luke didn't speak for a while after Franco left. He stood looking out over the terrace, brooding. 'It can't be true, can it?' he asked at last.

'He had the right names,' Hope said. 'It could be true about the child.'

'*Bastardo!*' Luke said again. 'She thinks he was so wonderful, and all the time—'

'But why are you angry?' she asked him. 'Surely this solves your problem?'

'How do you mean?'

'You wanted a way to drive him from her heart, and now you have it. Just tell her that the husband she idolised deceived her. Surely the simplest calculation should make that plain.'

'I don't like the word calculation,' he growled.

'It's the one you've always lived by. I was merely speaking your own language.'

'All right.' He swung round. 'Let's say I tell her about this woman and child because I've *calculated*—' he nearly spat the word '—that it will benefit me. But will it? It happened before he knew her, so where's the betrayal?'

'He went on seeing them when he came to Naples.'

'As any decent man would, rather than abandon his child. He kept quiet so as not to hurt her, but that still makes Minnie the one he truly loved. If I want to destroy him in her eyes, I'll need more than that.'

'But he went on sleeping with this woman,' Hope pointed out. 'There is the betrayal. Tell Minnie that. Make her accept the truth. Then the road should be clear for you.'

In silence he turned and looked at her.

*   *   *

Minnie's phone rang at exactly eleven o'clock.

'I waited until now so as not to interrupt your work,' Luke said.

'I might be asleep by now,' she pointed out.

'You never were. We were usually still talking nonsense at this hour. Then you'd make the cocoa.'

She laughed, and they fell silent.

'What are you doing now?' he asked.

'Just closing the books, then going to bed.'

Trying to put off the moment, she thought, *because it's so lonely without you.*

'You were supposed to be having some time off after that case collapsed,' he reminded her. 'You could have stayed here.'

'No, I—I don't think that would have been a good idea. There's too much... Things get confused.'

'Yes,' he said, and she knew that he, too, was remembering their last meeting alone, when he'd railed at Gianni's ghost.

'What about you?' she asked. 'What are you doing?'

'I went to the hospital with Mamma, for her to have a check-up. Everything's fine. And my bandages have been removed.'

'Is your arm better?'

'Looking good. I'll be back soon, driving you crazy.'

She thought, but didn't say, When?

'Franco's going back to Los Angeles at the end of the week.'

So it would be at least the end of the week before he would return. She forced her voice to be bright and cheerful, saying, 'I'm sure your mother wants him with her as much as possible before he vanishes again.'

'She was thrilled with the card you sent her, by the way.'

'She was so nice to me, I wanted to thank her, and wish her well.'

They talked for a few more minutes, saying nothing about the things that were really in their minds. When she had put the phone down the flat felt very quiet. It had always been quiet and lonely since Gianni died, but somehow this was different.

She took out his picture and settled down with it as she had done so often before.

'What do I do now?' she whispered. 'You were always a fast talker—go on, tell me.'

The smile in his eyes was as charming as ever, but now something was missing. There had always been a gleam, inviting her into the loving conspiracy they shared. Now it seemed to be gone. It was just a flat photograph. She tried again.

'I don't know whether I'm coming or going. No man ever did that to me before, not even you. You came on to me the very first evening, and I always knew what you were thinking. But now—'

She waited, hoping for what had happened before, that out of her memories would rise one that gave her the answer. But there was nothing, and she realised that Gianni couldn't help her with this.

In fact, there was no more help he could give her. The moment had been a long time coming, and she wasn't quite sure when he'd finally slipped away from her. Closing her eyes now, all she could feel was Luke's hand on her hair, and his whispered promise, 'I'm here.'

She opened her eyes again. Gianni's face was the same, unchanging, as it would always be now. She pressed her lips against the glass, realising finally how cold it was.

'Thank you for everything,' she whispered, 'all the years—thank you, thank you, my love. And goodbye.'

She put the picture away in her desk, and turned the key in the lock.

Luke called her every day. The calls were always the same—cheerful, non-committal, cautious. It was as though they were both waiting for something to happen.

Netta remained obstinately smiling, refusing to admit that her plans had suffered a setback. Minnie even found her going through a magazine full of wedding dresses.

'That one,' she said, pointing to a slender, elegant creation.

'I couldn't wear that,' Minnie said, outraged. 'It's bridal white, and I'm a widow.'

'So, there's a law against it?' Netta snorted. 'You wear what you like.'

'Only if I'm getting married, and I'm not. I wish I could make you understand that.'

'Pooh!' Netta said. 'It's written in your stars. You marry in Santa Maria in Trastevere—'

'Oh, so you've chosen the church as well as the dress! It's a pity we don't have a groom, but why be troubled by a detail?'

'I take care of the church and the dress,' Netta said. 'But I leave the groom to you.' She added, as a parting shot, 'You've gotta do *something* for yourself.'

Minnie glared but, since Netta took no notice whatever, she had no recourse but to depart and head back to her own home.

There was a man on the staircase, looking up and down and around, clearly lost.

'Can I help you?' Minnie asked.

He turned, smiling. Something in that smile sent a *fris-*

son of alarm through her, although she couldn't, at that moment, have said why.

Ten minutes later she knew the worst, and was running down the stairs to find her car and head out of Rome, hell-bent for Naples.

The family had been to see Franco off at the airport, and had enjoyed a good dinner on their return home. Now the Villa Rinucci was closing down for the night, and Luke and his mother were taking a last walk around the garden.

'It's been wonderful to see Franco,' Hope said wistfully, 'but it's probably a good thing if he's not around while you're sorting things out with Minnie.'

'Yes, he knows too much,' Luke agreed wryly.

'Have you decided yet what you're going to tell her?'

'No, I have no idea.'

'It's been nearly a week. I don't recall when I've seen you so indecisive.'

'I keep thinking it's simple. I'll tell her, because I can't live out the future keeping such a secret from her. But then I think what it will do to her, and I know I can never say anything.'

'Even if it means living with Saint Gianni for ever? Could you do that?'

'I don't know.' He added lightly, 'I suppose, if we're married, it's always possible that she might turn her thoughts to me occasionally. I'm not asking for miracles, but, hey—it might happen.'

She laughed and patted his arm. 'You're becoming a realist, my son.'

They had reached the front of the house and he stopped, looking down the hill to where he could see moving lights.

'What is it?' Hope asked.

'Someone's heading towards us at a great rate.'

They watched the fast moving lights winding up the hill until Luke said, 'Surely, that's Minnie's car?'

'I think it is,' Hope said, unable to keep the pleasure and excitement out of her voice.

The car came to a halt with a screech and Minnie was out in a moment, slamming the door behind her and advancing on Luke with a face of doom. The lamps showed tears glistening on her face.

'*You!*' she said, pointing at him. 'I knew it! *I knew it!* I should never have trusted you from the first moment, but you made me feel sorry for you and I swear I'll never feel sorry for anyone again as long as I live. I trusted you, more fool me!'

Luke finally got his breath. 'Minnie, will you please tell me what this is all about?'

'I'll tell you in two words,' she raged. '*Eduardo Viccini!*'

His groan and the way he closed his eyes in despair told her all she needed to know.

'You do know the man I'm talking about, don't you?' she snapped.

'Yes, I know. I gather you've met him.'

'Yes, I've met him. He came looking for you today and said some very interesting things. You should have been more careful, Luke. You should have warned him that I knew nothing about the interesting little scheme the two of you had cooked up. You lying, treacherous, two-faced—'

She broke off as more tears came, furiously brushing them away, trying to deny them, but unable to stop because she felt as though something was crushing her heart.

'Minnie—' He reached out to her but she flung his hand aside.

'Don't come near me.'

'Look, I'm sorry you met him like that—'

'You're sorry I met him at all. At least, you are if you've got any sense. I wasn't supposed to find out that you were planning to betray the lot of us until it was too late, was I?'

There was careful movement inside the house as the sounds of altercation brought the rest of the family to doors and windows, but silently. Nobody wanted to miss this, certainly not Primo and Olympia, who stood, arms entwined, watching the last act of a drama that was partly their own. Hope melted softly into the shadows.

'I have not betrayed you,' Luke said. 'Any of you.'

'Oh, I suppose it isn't betrayal to sell out to a development company—'

'I haven't—'

'Don't lie to me,' she cried. 'You'll be telling me next that you've never heard of Allerio Proprieta.'

'I've done more than heard of it. I formed it. Allerio Proprieta is me, with some backing from Eduardo Viccini. I'm the boss but I need his finance. What I'm planning is going to be expensive.'

'I'll bet it is, starting with clearing the whole lot of us out.'

'No, I swear it. Everyone who wants to stay is safe. You've said yourself that I can't force anyone out, and I'm not trying to. Offering them sweeteners is another matter.'

'You admit it?'

'I don't admit anything,' Luke said, 'because I've done nothing wrong. If a man has something I want I'll offer him a fair price for it. He's free to say no, and if he does he'll get no trouble from me. If he says yes, it's because he's gaining something, and that is fair exchange.'

'Some of them are leaving already. You must have worked damned hard to bring that about.'

'You mean Mario in number eight? He's been offered a good job on the other side of Rome and he wants to live close to it. It's a promotion, so he can afford a bigger home, which is fine because his wife is pregnant.'

'And I suppose it's coincidence that he was offered that job now?'

'Coincidence, nothing! Eduardo knows someone who's always looking for people with Mario's skills. Their meeting was a success, and now Mario has the job of his dreams. Do you think he feels ill-used? I promise you he doesn't.'

While she tried to find an answer to this, Luke went on, 'What about the couple in number twenty-three? They want to stop renting and buy, but they haven't got the deposit for the place they want. Or rather, they didn't have.'

'And you gave it to them?'

'No, I'm not Santa Claus, it's an interest free loan, and now they're happy as skylarks. If you don't believe me, ask them.

'I could give you a dozen other cases. They're not all attached to the Residenza as we are. For them it's just a place to live for a while, then pass on. I'm just making it easy for them to do that.'

'And what about my family?'

'They'll stay. Anyone who wants to can stay, but plenty will leave, willingly, and I can start work, making it a smart place to live.'

She was silent, confused and troubled. One thing he'd said was flashing in her mind.

'What do you mean, *we*?' she asked.

'We?'

'You said, "They're not all attached to the Residenza as *we* are." *We?*'

'Yes, I love it. I plan to live there. That's why Pietro is moving out of the flat next to mine, and into a small one lower down. Boy, did that cost me! I need both those flats so that I can knock them into one and have a place that's big enough for two people.'

'For—two?'

'Yes, I don't think that you and I can live in your present home. Better to make a fresh start in our own place.'

'Whoa, you're going too fast for me. Who said we were going to live together?'

Luke drew a deep breath. 'Well, people who marry usually do that.'

'And who said we were going to get married?'

'Netta said it. And Charlie said it, and Tomaso said it, and every single person in your family said it. But they only said it because Netta said it first. Now I'm saying it. It only needs you to say it, and everybody's said it.'

'Wait a minute!' She held up a hand to stop him. 'Are you proposing that we get married just because Netta's given her orders?'

'Why not? Your mother-in-law is exactly like my mother. People do what she says, sooner or later. Face it, Minnie! Netta had it sorted on the first day, so we may as well give in now.'

She stared at him, aghast.

'And that's a proposal is it? That's the great romantic proposal?'

'Well, I'm not at my best in front of an audience,' he said, jerking his head to include the crowd standing behind him, grinning now and relishing every moment.

'You—you've got a nerve—you dare—'

'I'm just doing as I'm told. You know I'm right about Netta. It wouldn't surprise me if she's actually decided on the church. She's probably even picked your wedding dress. What is it?'

Minnie had gasped and clapped her hands over her mouth.

'Minnie—what is it?'

She couldn't answer. The eerie accuracy of his prediction had taken her breath away. It was as though fate had tapped her on the shoulder and said, This way!

'Santa Maria in Trastevere,' she whispered.

'Is that the church where we're marrying?'

'Netta says so.'

'Has she fixed the date?'

'Probably—*Luke!*'

'Come here,' he said fiercely, and pulled her towards him.

In the long, long kiss that followed the rest of the Rinucci family emerged slowly and quietly, until they were standing on the porch, watching with pleasure the two who were embracing in the patch of light below. Only Hope stood a little apart, holding her breath for the issue that she knew was still to be resolved.

'How could you think I'd stoop so low?' he asked when he finally released her.

'I don't know, but it was the worst thing that ever happened to me. I trusted you.'

'That's not what you used to say,' he said wryly.

'Not to your face, maybe, but I always knew you were decent and honest, no matter how many insults I hurled at you. And then, when I thought you'd cheated us—it was as though the central pillar of the world had cracked. Until then, I didn't know how much I minded. Luke, don't you understand, it's the most terrible thing that can happen, to trust someone you love and then find out they were betraying you?'

'Yes,' he said softly. 'I do understand that. And that's why—' he was holding her hands tightly '—there's something I have to say to you, and I want you to listen well, because it's important.'

'Yes?' She was looking at him with shining eyes.

'I told you once that I'd never make love to you until I came first.'

'But you do come first—in my heart—in my whole life—'

'First among the living, but I wanted to drive out his ghost.'

'Luke—'

'It's all right; let me finish. I wanted to get rid of Gianni, but I was being selfish. I was jealous of him. He gave you ten years of happiness, and who knows if I can measure up to that? I guess I just didn't like the competition, so I wanted to deprive you of the sweetest memories you have, all to suit my convenience.

'Try to forgive me for that, because I see more clearly now. One love doesn't drive out another. Nor should it. Keep your ghost, my darling. Keep him and go right on loving him as he deserved. I dare say I can manage to live in a threesome.'

Every eye was fixed on them. Nobody noticed that Hope's face was transformed by a smile of pride in her son.

Minnie looked intently at Luke. 'Do you have anything else to say?'

'Nothing.'

'Does that mean you're not going to tell me?'

'Tell you what?'

'About Elsa Alessio,' she said simply.

He stared, truly shocked.

'What do you know about that?'

'I know that she's a woman in Naples who bore Gianni's son, years ago, before he met me. He used to see them when he drove his truck down here. He was a good father, but I was the one he loved.'

'He told you—everything?' he asked, hardly daring to believe.

'Of course he did. We loved each other. He wouldn't have deceived me. He told me everything that I needed to know,' she added with a slightly ambiguous phrasing that he didn't notice until later.

He could hardly believe that he'd been let off the hook. Or at least, almost. There was still one tiny hook.

It was on the tip of his tongue to ask if she believed Gianni had been faithful to her on those visits to Elsa. Did she know that he had boasted otherwise?

But the next moment he knew that this was a secret he must keep. Who could tell if such boasts had been true, or even if he'd said any such thing? And, without certainty, he had no right to speak.

And if the worst was true, and she had to learn it one day, he would prepare for that day by making her so happy in their marriage that nothing from the past could touch her.

That was the resolve he made to himself, that he would keep in secret and never speak of to her as long as they both lived.

'Would you really move to Rome, for me?' she asked in wonder.

'I can extend my business there, and become a sleeping partner in the Naples factories. I'll enjoy the challenge of new territories. You can't leave your practice. You've built it up in Rome.'

'And you're not jealous of it?' There was an old anxiety in her voice.

'I swear I'll never be jealous. Or at least, if I am,' he added with a touch of humour, 'I'll keep it decently to myself.'

She reached up and took his head between her hands, searching his face.

'When I thought I'd lost you, it was the end of the world for me. I love you so much; without you there's nothing.'

'Don't say it unless you're completely sure,' he said anxiously.

'Completely, totally, utterly sure. I thought I could never love any other man again, but I was only waiting for you. I didn't want to believe it—I got so mad at you—'

'Yes, I know that,' he said with a laugh that sounded shaky because relief and happiness were making him weak. 'I tried to get mad at you, but I could barely manage it, and I could never stay mad for five minutes. You used to look at me in that way you have, and then—I don't know—things happened to me.'

'I think it's time something happened now,' she murmured, tightening her hands on his head.

In the long kiss that followed they could hear the sound of soft cheering from the shadows.

'My family are just loving this,' he murmured.

Then he was silent, holding her fiercely against him, as though afraid to risk her slipping away, kissing her again and again.

'Do I hear applause?' she murmured.

'Probably. The Rinuccis are like the Pepinos. Love and marriage concern everyone. All those things they heard me say once, about keeping control of my life, being cautious, even in love—what a laugh I'm giving them now! But I don't care. Let them laugh, because I'm the winner. *Carissima,* I don't want to keep control of my life any longer. I want you to have it. Take it, and keep me safe.'

'There's something I want you to know,' she said earnestly.

'What is it, my love?'

'I said goodbye to Gianni yesterday, finally and for good. He understands.'

It was said afterwards that the meeting of Netta Pepino and Hope Rinucci was like the meeting of monarchs. An official visit was made from Naples to Rome, and the Rinuccis were ceremonially entertained.

Hope and Netta inspected the two flats that were being knocked into one and pronounced themselves satisfied.

'You have done the right thing in choosing to live in Rome,' Hope told him privately later. They were standing at the window in Netta's front room, eating her delicious home-made cake. 'Franco will be home soon, and it's best not to risk him saying a word out of turn.'

'I nearly said it myself,' he observed.

'Oh, no,' Hope said fondly. 'You were never going to tell her anything.'

'You can't be sure of that.'

'Certainly I'm sure. You love her far too much to hurt her. I always knew that. But I wasn't sure that *you* knew.'

'I didn't know, until I was faced with the choice. Then I realised there was no choice. There never had been. But you—all that stuff you were handing me about calculating how to get what I wanted—'

'My son, I knew you wouldn't actually do it. I know you better than you know yourself.'

Toni, who'd been standing behind them for the last minute, observed, 'Even so, I think he can still surprise you.'

'How do you mean, *caro*?'

'Tell her, Luke.'

'Years ago Toni offered me the chance to become a Rinucci, and I turned it down because there was still a lot about families that I didn't understand. An hour ago I asked him if the offer was still open.'

'And I told him it was,' Toni said.

He was right. Hope was taken utterly by surprise. Her eyes filled with tears of joy and she embraced the son who had finally decided to come in from the cold.

The only person not pleased by this arrangement was Netta.

'Better you change your name to Pepino,' she advised him. 'Then you'll be descended from an emperor.'

Laughing, Luke vetoed the idea, but Netta had her own way in everything else. Minnie wore the slim white dress and veil for her wedding in Santa Maria in Trastevere, and afterwards she and her groom went in a horse-drawn carriage through the streets to the Residenza, where the reception was to be held in the courtyard.

The carriage took the long way round, for the sake of all her neighbours who wanted to see her, and by the time it reached home the families had contrived to get there first, climbing the stairs, hung with fresh white flowers, until they lined the inner surface of the courtyard, almost to the sky.

Netta and Hope, two queens, led the cheers that broke

out as they appeared under the arch into the courtyard, and when hundreds of white petals showered down on the bride and groom as they stood gazing upwards in wonder, it was they who threw the first and the last, and they who cheered, laughed and wept the longest.

If you enjoyed what you just read,
then we've got an offer you can't resist!

Take 2 bestselling love stories FREE!

Plus get a FREE surprise gift!

Clip this page and mail it to Harlequin Reader Service®

IN U.S.A.
3010 Walden Ave.
P.O. Box 1867
Buffalo, N.Y. 14240-1867

IN CANADA
P.O. Box 609
Fort Erie, Ontario
L2A 5X3

YES! Please send me 2 free Harlequin Romance® novels and my free surprise gift. After receiving them, if I don't wish to receive anymore, I can return the shipping statement marked cancel. If I don't cancel, I will receive 6 brand-new novels every month, before they're available in stores! In the U.S.A., bill me at the bargain price of $3.57 plus 25¢ shipping & handling per book and applicable sales tax, if any*. In Canada, bill me at the bargain price of $4.05 plus 25¢ shipping & handling per book and applicable taxes**. That's the complete price and a savings of 10% off the cover prices—what a great deal! I understand that accepting the 2 free books and gift places me under no obligation ever to buy any books. I can always return a shipment and cancel at any time. Even if I never buy another book from Harlequin, the 2 free books and gift are mine to keep forever.

186 HDN DZ72
386 HDN DZ73

Name	(PLEASE PRINT)	
Address	Apt.#	
City	State/Prov.	Zip/Postal Code

Not valid to current Harlequin Romance® subscribers.
Want to try another series? Call 1-800-873-8635
or visit www.morefreebooks.com.

* Terms and prices subject to change without notice. Sales tax applicable in N.Y.
** Canadian residents will be charged applicable provincial taxes and GST.
   All orders subject to approval. Offer limited to one per household.
   ® are registered trademarks owned and used by the trademark owner and or its licensee.

HROM04R   ©2004 Harlequin Enterprises Limited

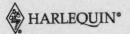
Coming Next Month

#3891 THE CATTLE BARON'S BRIDE Margaret Way
Men of the Outback

Cattleman Ross Sunderland wouldn't have agreed to be the guide for the Northern Territory trip if he'd known delicate city beauty Samantha Langdon had signed up. Their one meeting had sparked an overwhelming attraction, and loner Ross had vowed to avoid her at all costs. But now—seduced by the danger and primitive beauty around them—can they still deny their passion…?

#3892 MEANT-TO-BE MARRIAGE Rebecca Winters

When Jarod Kendall met beautiful Sydney Taylor, he faced the hardest decision of his life. He was a priest, and any relationship was forbidden. After a year of Jarod hiding his feelings, Sydney left town, believing her love wasn't returned. But now Jarod is determined to find her, and persuade her that against all the odds their marriage is meant to be….

#3893 THE FIVE-YEAR BABY SECRET Liz Fielding

Fleur Gilbert and Matt Hanover married in secret, believing their love could end a family feud. They were wrong. Six lonely years later, Matt has never forgotten Fleur. And when he discovers that their one-night marriage created a son he never knew he had, he's determined to claim his child—and his wife….

#3894 ORDINARY GIRL, SOCIETY GROOM Natasha Oakley

Eloise Lawson has finally found the family she's never known. But now, cast adrift in the high-society world, there's only one person she can depend on: broodingly handsome Jeremy Norland. Eloise realizes that if she falls in love with him she's in danger of losing everything she's fought so hard to find. Will she have the courage to risk all?